STRONGLY WORDED WOMEN

The Best of the Year of Publishing Women: An Anthology

Edited by Sydney Culpepper

Published in the United States by Not a Pipe Publishing, Independence, Oregon. www.NotAPipePublishing.com

Trade Paperback Edition
ISBN-13: 978-1-948120-24-1

Dedicated to all the women
whose stories have yet gone unread.
May we read those tales soon.

Letter from the Editor

One question that Not a Pipe Publishing has received many times since taking on Kamila Shamsie's challenge to make 2018 the Year of Publishing Women is "Why?" My response is, "Why not?" Why are some people so afraid of a Year of Publishing Women when we've already had Centuries of Publishing Men?

When one looks at the 'classics' of literature that are taught in school, who do we see? We see William Shakespeare and George Orwell; Edgar Allen Poe and Leo Tolstoy; and the list of white men continues. In contrast, how many classic women authors are there? Only Jane Austen and the Brontë sisters come to the forefront of most minds, with the occasional Mary Shelley or Virginia Woolf.

It is an undeniable fact that the publishing industry had favored works by white men for centuries. This a result of the patriarchal, white-centric society that has thrived in most parts of the world. It is the result of a lack of equal rights and education, not a result of inherent talent.

Yes, these male authors and books shaped the world; I don't disagree. However, I invite you to think about how many books by women and people of color could have also shaped the world if only they'd been given the tools, education, and time.

I will step off my soap box now to say this: I am deeply

grateful to Not a Pipe Publishing for taking on the Year of Publishing Women, and for giving me this project to lead. Companies like Not a Pipe and people like the Gormans give me hope for our world, because a diverse world that celebrates all of its voices is a better world.

I have been so humbled by the many story submissions we received throughout the year, and I'm so grateful this short story project was a success. When I was selecting which stories to include in the anthology—not an easy series of decisions in the slightest—I kept thinking about a theme to center the anthology around, but I kept hitting a wall.

All of these stories are as unique and individual as the authors who wrote them, and I struggled to come up with a unifying theme until I realized the strength behind each piece. You will notice that each one of them has a message or element of strength behind it that will blow you away and destroy any doubts you have about the power of women.

No longer will women and people of color and members of other marginalized communities be kept silent. We will fight for our words and our stories, because we can change the world too.

—Sydney Culpepper, Editor

Table of Contents

Content Warnings

We have chosen to provide these general content warnings to help readers feel safe and comfortable while enjoying the anthology. This is not an exhaustive list of all possible triggers.

Blaise
Brief hate speech, mentions of rape and sexual abuse, mention of incestual child abuse, physical assault.

Pack Mentality
Mentions of mental and emotional child abuse.

Mother Nature…Mother Nurture
Mental illness, death and dying.

Eyes
Body horror.

Maiden Voyage of the Fearless
Mental illness.

Skin-Deep
Implied human trafficking, enslavement, mental and physical abuse, mention of rape, suicide.

The Woman Against the Window
Sexual assault/non-consent.

Getting Pregnant on the Back of a Motorcycle

Maren Bradley Anderson

I never figured out how Ellen and Eddy got together. My last trip home I saw them sitting on the back of his bike eating ice cream at the Freezee drive-in. How lame is it to be eating ice-cream at the Freezee when you're, like, 28? I was home visiting Mom, building her a porch instead of taking a real vacation somewhere that wasn't my shitty hometown.

Ellen had grown her hair longer, so the curls sprang in ten directions, but otherwise, she was as luscious as she had been at graduation. And she licked that cone like she wanted to have its babies.

Eddy ate his ice cream like he didn't trust it.

I nearly crashed Mom's Passat into the car in front of me while watching Ellen eat. Genius. Then I flipped a bitch into the Freezee parking lot and pulled in next to them. Double Genius.

But she was mine first. Those blue eyes and that curly black hair? Mine. Crooked front tooth? Mine. Diabolical mind? On my side first.

Eddy was a whiny little shit with money and no spine. He tried to make up for it by riding a very loud motorcycle. It's not a Harley—he's not that cool—just a knock-off rice grinder. I'd kicked his ass a couple times when we were kids for being a snotty little shit. Maybe that's why he's always been a dick to me. Maybe he's just an asshat.

I don't know what I expected when I opened the car door, but I didn't expect the blank look under Ellen's precisely arched brows. Like hunting bows.

I wasn't surprised by Eddy's reaction, though.

"Hey, asshole. What do you want?"

"Ice cream." Then I said, "Ellen? You don't remember me."

She made a show of squinting at me and then threw back her head and laughed just the way she used to in high school when we'd talk about someone she didn't like.

"Justus!" she cried, with a half-smile. "How the hell are you?"

I should have said, "Fine," and walked away. I knew that look. At least, I did at one time.

Instead, I said, "I'm great. How the hell are you?"

She tossed her head again, her hair flying and a chain on her motorcycle jacket jangling. "Oh, you know. Still stuck in this town. Working. Having fun." She nudged Eddy with an elbow.

"What do you want, Justus?" Eddy slid an arm around Ellen's waist, and she wiggled closer to him.

But she locked eyes with me and took a huge bite of ice cream, leading with her teeth. Her crooked tooth made my toes tingle.

"Just to say hi," I said. "In town at my mom's. Thought I'd see some friends."

"Wanna come out with us tonight?" Ellen asked.

"What?" Eddy and I both asked.

"Why not?" she said. "Catch up on old times, right?" She bit the cone again and fluttered her eyelashes first at me, then at Eddy.

Eddy was glaring at me, trying to intimidate me, I suppose, but I wasn't paying attention. Why would I? I had once held him face-down in a muddy puddle, and my former girlfriend was now giving me come-hither eyes.

"Sounds good," I said. "I'm game for anything."

Maybe this would be a good time to state that I did have my reservations about actually meeting up with them. I wasn't the most wholesome person in the world, but Ellen...Ellen was what her closest friends call "a piece of work." I reminded myself that Ellen's idea of comeuppance for the boyfriend before me was to steal his truck's distributor cap and then spread the rumor that his penis was three inches long. His sin? He couldn't make the prom because his grandmother's funeral was the same day.

Our relationship didn't end well, either. Senior year, I got an acceptance letter to an out-of-state college, and she didn't. Somehow that was my fault. One summer and two sets of slashed tires later, I went to school and she stayed here.

Still, after a day of rebuilding Mom's porch, I showered, shaved, and drove to the Alibi, the bar we used to sneak into with our fake ID's. The place still held an element of danger for me. The fact that Ellen suggested the Alibi made the "you're getting away with something" vibe even stronger.

It was one of those bars that never changes. In the 1970's, someone decided it would be groovy to tile every vertical surface with colored, mirrored glass. The shadowbox was mirrored, too, and all the horizontal lines—bar top, stools, tables—were painted black. Very psychedelic. Very dated. Awesomely Retro, or cheap, depending on your perspective. It was where I'd go when I was in town to act out with my friends, even though the 'Niner's posters were peeling off the walls and the black Naugahyde on the stools was wearing thin.

It was Thursday, and kids from Humboldt State were there. I wasn't surprised when I didn't recognize the bartender, but she'd been working there long enough to know that a plunging neckline brings bigger tips. She told me she hadn't seen Ellen yet, but she knew her. I was awarded a wink with my beer. "Where'd you meet Ellen?"

"High school."

"So, I don't need to warn you?"

I grinned and turned my beer around slowly on the coaster. "I probably need a refresher."

"She's trouble."

"Yes, she is." I looked up at her. "What kind of trouble do you mean?"

"I mean the kind of trouble cute boys like you don't want to be part of."

I laughed. "You don't know me very well, miss."

"No," she said, drawing the "O" out with a puckered lip. "I don't, do I?"

Then, for some reason, she stroked my hand and walked to the other end of the bar.

A few minutes later, she caught my eye and pointed to the door. Ellen's graceful silhouette was in the doorway peering into the shadows. She was looking for me. I reveled in this knowledge for a moment before waving to her.

She smiled and walked towards me, alone.

"Hi!" She threw her arms around my neck, rubbing every part of her against me.

"Where's Eddy?" I asked her hair.

"Who cares?" she said, arranging herself onto a stool.

The bartender set a napkin in front of Ellen but looked at me. "What are you drinking, El?"

"Usual, Bev." Ellen didn't take her eyes off me, either.

A moment later, Bev slid a tall drink across the bar, and I slid a ten back. "Keep it."

Bev put a finger on the back of my hand as she took the bill so I would look up at her. She smiled and tucked a napkin under my palm. I wadded it up with one hand, and she moved away.

"Do you know her?" Ellen asked.

Did she see anything more than a meaningful look? I said, "No. Cute, huh?"

Ellen narrowed her eyes.

"Gotcha," I said.

She laughed without preamble, and I did, too. "You still like teasing the tiger. You always did." She purred and dragged a fingernail up my thigh.

I took her hand. It was cold. I almost put it down again.

"How many years has it been?" I asked.

She shrugged. "Too many." She touched my face with her other hand and looked in my eyes. "You haven't changed at all."

"You're more beautiful."

She smiled. "Let's go somewhere."

"Don't you want to 'catch up'?"

She snorted, an unpleasant habit I remembered from high school. "Talk. Talk is cheap."

"Still," I said. "Talk to me."

She grumbled and fidgeted, using that lickable lower lip of hers to pout.

"What are you doing nowadays?" I asked.

She sat back and crossed her arms. Then she uncrossed them and took a long draw from her drink. "Let's catch you up," she said. "I dropped out of junior college sophomore year. Got pregnant on the back of a motorcycle. Had a baby. Did some time for DUI. Lost the baby to the state. Now I shuffle paper at a veterinary clinic. It's a promotion from cleaning the cages. So, how's your life been?"

"Jesus, I'm sorry," I said.

"Yeah, me, too." She pulled a cigarette out of my shirt pocket and lit up with her own lighter. The bartender simply put an ashtray in front of her. I eyed the "No Smoking" sign and then pulled a smoke out for myself.

"On the back of a motorcycle?" I asked. My mind instantly flickered to Eddy's bike.

Ellen was watching me. "Yeah."

"That must have been tricky."

"You want me to draw you a diagram?"

"I'll just let my imagination run wild, if you don't mind." We grinned at each other.

"So?" she prompted.

"Oh, my life. Umm. Wife and three kids. I like my job..."

"What do you do?"

"Astronaut." I laughed when she choked on her drink. "Just fucking with you. I do boring office shit that no one finds interesting except me."

"Three kids?" It was dark, but her face looked a little softer, maybe.

"Joey, Ashley, Ben."

"Lucky bastard." She stabbed out her half-smoked cigarette. "Three kids."

"Yeah." I took her hand again.

She looked at me. I watched as the soft look took on familiar hard corners. Her hand was still cold.

"Are we done catching up, yet?" she asked.

"I think so."

As we stood up, Eddy walked through the door and squinted into the dark.

* * *

I didn't know where we were going. I was only following the loud growling of the bike and its single tail light because just above it was Ellen's perfect ass. Eddy was in as foul a mood as before, but he let her lead him to his bike and tell him where to go. I followed in Mom's robin's-egg Passat down deserted roads that were hauntingly familiar in the dark. Whispers of things I did in the woods back in high school tickled the back of my head.

I had time to reflect on our conversation. The "three kids" lie was almost as outrageous as the astronaut story. To have a wife and three kids would necessitate my having married someone. So far, marriage was as unlikely as my getting into the NASA training program. Well, maybe not *that* unlikely. I pulled out the wadded napkin and read Bev's number again. She wasn't as cute as Ellen, but few people were. However, Bev was probably not Ellen's equal in a lot of respects, which was a good thing. I put the number face down on the dash and set Mom's box of tissues on top of it. I'd learned long ago not to assume stuff in my wallet was safe from Ellen.

I also learned long ago not to trust Ellen's stories. For example: no one gets pregnant on the back of a motorcycle. That was a totally Ellen-esque invention. I admired the quality of her lie, though; I had instantly wondered if Eddy was the father and felt the intended flare of jealousy. Now I wondered if there even was a baby. I hadn't heard that she'd had a kid from any of my high school friends, and news like that certainly would have found its way to me.

The single tail light slowed and turned into a pull-out. Soon, I stood at the head of a trail that led down a hill listening to a river rush far below. Ellen came to stand next to me, grinning like a shark, and then plunged into the darkness.

"Stay on the path!" she called over her shoulder.

Eddy shoved past me, so I followed, overcoming my urge to push him into the dirt at the bottom of the hill.

It was so dark I couldn't see them ahead of me, though I could hear their footsteps and Eddy cursing when a branch swatted his face. I realized the water I had heard was the Mad river, which skirted the edge of town. Ellen and Eddy were crashing through the forest, her laugh dancing around the trunks of the trees, but I could still hear the spring peepers—tiny frogs—and an owl above their din. There was a smell, too, mixed in with the forest scent of earth and fir. I couldn't quite place it, but it was sticky-sweet and green.

Eventually, there was a light ahead. As I got closer, I saw it was a tiny shack with one glowing window. I opened the door and was bathed in warm light bouncing off a copper still. In the rafters, stalks of pot were drying. The smell—green, sweet, sticky—hit me again. I grinned.

Ellen was on a tattered mattress in the corner, holding a jar of clear liquid and taking a hit off a newly-lit joint. Eddy pulled off his shirt—man, he was pasty and hairy—and then turned to the still. I closed the door.

"Here." Eddy shoved a jar into my hands.

I sniffed it. "Moonshine?"

"White dog whiskey, asshole," he said. "It's a new thing."

"It's not going to make me go blind, is it?"

Ellen laughed and made a show of downing the rest of her jar. "See? Good stuff," she said between coughing spasms. She held her arm high above her to keep the smoking joint safe.

The moonshine burned my throat in a bad way. I shook my head and whooped. "I like how you kids party around here."

Eddy actually smiled. "Granddad's still. I've been perfecting the mash for years." He took the joint from Ellen, took a long drag, then handed it to me.

"Perfect," I said.

I looked at Ellen over the good, sweet smoke. She met my eyes and pulled off her shirt and bra in one movement. Eddy downed the rest of his mason jar and flopped next to her on the mattress.

"Dude," he said. "No Bogarting."

Well, what was I going to do? I knocked back the rest of the moonshine, put the joint in my teeth, and unbuttoned my shirt. I wasn't nearly drunk or high enough to feel good about this decision, but I wasn't leaving, and watching was not an option. That only left one thing to do. I sat next to them on the mattress and gave Ellen the joint.

"You haven't changed since high school, have you?" Ellen purred. Eddy set his glasses on a windowsill and then kissed her neck, ignoring me. Ellen dropped the joint into an ashtray while she slid her other hand under my open shirt and smiled. Eddy bit her, and she yelped and giggled.

She pulled me down and shoved Eddy to the side. Her taste brought back all those old feelings: anger, rebellion, lust, danger. I slid my tongue over her tooth and moaned. Her fingers in my hair, wringing something from my head. She pulled me back and looked me in the eye. Maybe it was the pot or the moonshine, but her face smeared in front of me.

Then, I was in the backseat of my beloved '69 Mustang with her, both eighteen, trying to explain why I was leaving town even while fresh hickeys stung on our necks.

"College," I said. "So I can get out of here. So I don't have to work at the mill."

"My daddy and uncle work at the mill," she sniffed.

"I don't want to," I said. "I want a real job. In an office."

"Don't you want me?"

"Yes, but..."

"'Cause, I'm not leaving."

"I'll come back."

"You won't," she said. "No one does."

I couldn't deny that I wanted to look out a window and see something other than the mill pouring noxious white smoke into the sky. I wanted to forget the shrill whistle that called the workers like cattle to their slots in the factory. I couldn't tell her what she wanted to hear, so I didn't say anything.

"You'll go somewhere else, get married, and whatever," she said. "But you'll always be fucking Justus!"

She slammed the door so hard the glass rattled in the jamb.

On the mattress in the shack, she pressed her nails into my scalp, and I wondered if she was trying to draw blood. There was something very ugly in her look. Destructive. Inviting, but not wholesome. She was so incredibly sexy.

She knew it. Her lips parted, and I could see her pink tongue and crooked tooth, and I almost dove in again. I knew, I remembered the darkness, I would willingly sink into that well. It was familiar, but...

What does she want?

"I'm glad you're here, Mr. 'Three kids and a wife.'"

Oh. Right. Revenge.

I stood and had almost buttoned my shirt before Ellen said my name.

"Justus?"

I glanced back from the door. Eddy was on top of her now, one hand over her mouth, another cupping a breast, and he squinted at me with a sloppy grin. Ellen was watching me, not fighting him. I wondered how far she would have gone this time if I had stayed. I closed the door.

I walked back more slowly, not thinking about where to go, just going. I stepped carefully around the pot plants

I had crashed through before. I listened to the little frogs and the crickets. I watched the treetops catch the thin, lacy clouds that held the moonlight and kept it from reaching me down on the ground. I knew enough to stay on the path; Eddy was the kind of fuckhead who would booby-trap a marijuana patch.

At the foot of the hill below the road, I sat and looked back toward the sound of the stony river. I thought of Bev's number on the dashboard and allowed myself the fantasy of calling her now and taking her somewhere private where she'd screw my brains out and make me forget the picture of Ellen looking at me with Eddy's hand over her face. I imagined myself marrying the flirty bartender in Barbados and not inviting anyone from this town.

I looked at the motorcycle when I got to the top of the hill. I leaned against my mother's car, smoked a cigarette, and really looked at that machine. I imagined the two of them walking back to town in the morning, him pushing while she complained. It was a very good picture.

But what would I be paying them back for? Him for being with Ellen, the girl who taught me self-loathing and who made all successive women sweet and charming by comparison? Her for trying to break up my fictional family?

No. They both deserved to suffer for reminding me.

Fictional kids and wife and astronaut job

notwithstanding, I am, really, no better than either of them. That's why I took the spark plugs.

I let the air out of the tires because sometimes I'm just a mean little fuck.

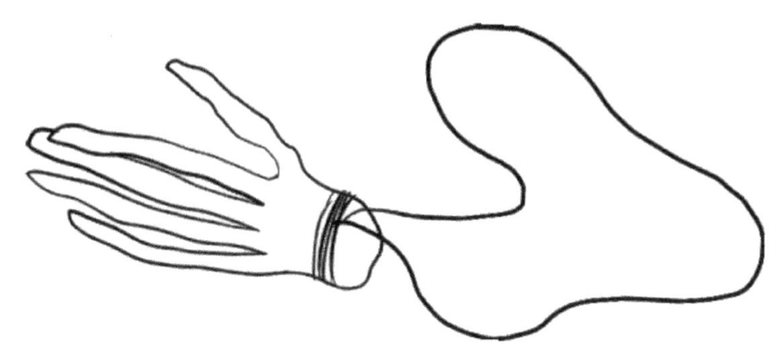

Beast

Debby Dodds

Washing mud out of my pubic hair had to be the worst part of this Renaissance Faire gig. But as mud-beggars, our fringe benefits rocked. We got a regular paycheck, but our contract with the Faire producers also allowed us to beseech money directly from the patrons. It was all part of setting the authentic "interactive improvisation" atmosphere, so that over-fed, under-educated, middle-American losers could feel like they'd "stepped back in time for a day to 1589 in a small shire in Merry 'ole England."

Usually after our four daily mud-shows, with titles like A Mud-summer's Night Dream, The Duchess of Mudpies, and The Muddy Wives of Windsor, the three of us mud-beggars pulled in close to an extra $200 a day each from audience tips. Most of the other actors in the cast of the Ren Faire were jealous of us. Sometimes I wasn't sure the extra money was really worth it. I think I'd have been happier playing a Pirate or Jester or a Lord of something. It was harder to flirt with the hot chicks when covered with mud. The royal fruity bastards who were part of the Queen's Court had all the gorgeous babes falling all over themselves to snuggle close for pictures. Not me. I had to take lots of pictures with snotty little kids and smelly old people. By the end of the summer, I tried to avoid getting my face muddy as long as I could, so I could still woo the lady patrons who were worth wooing. Putting our faces in the mud always generated more tips, so my fellow mud-beggars made more green than I did those days. But there are more important things than money. Like sex. Besides, I'd saved up plenty of money.

I didn't live extravagantly over the summer like some actors did, with their daytrips to Hershey Park to ride the roller coasters or midweek vacations to the shore to scarf the saltwater taffy. I always preferred riding women to riding machines and eating bearded clams to eating fried clams, anyway. Because of my smart choices, I'd saved enough to pay for my first few months' rent in an apartment in New York City while I looked for a job. Not that I cared, but my cold bitch of a mom would have approved of my thriftiness that summer. Unlike my dad, who used to pay for every round at the local bar, I made sure to be scarce when any check came. My dad had too big a heart, and where did that get him? Dead from a heart attack. I was pretty sure I inherited my lack of capacity for generosity and kindness from my mom. But I figured maybe I'd live a little longer because I was stingy like her.

As the summer drew to a close, my biggest problem was that the apartment I was planning on moving to next week had disappeared. Well, it was not exactly gone, but the asshole that I was going to move in with took back his offer. Turns out this guy's sister knew one of the actresses at the Faire that I got down and dirty with—this dancer chick with the ability to put her ankles behind her ears. We had a fun two weeks, but then she couldn't get over our break-up when her turn with me was up. Sorry, but it's not in my nature to nurture. So she whined to her friend, who put the screws to her brother to dump me. So now I was shit out of luck with my housing situation. Great.

I looked over at the cheap fake monkey paw talisman lying on my dresser. The fortune teller at the Faire had given me as a thank you gift after I'd had an impromptu threesome with her and the lady who sold the turkey legs. She'd told me it would grant wishes. I wasn't superstitious; I made my own luck. But what the hell, Why not? I grabbed it and wished that I'd find a roommate in New York City with a to-die-for apartment. Then I threw my little good luck charm into the duffle I'd been packing.

I knew I wasn't staying any longer than I had to in this crappy town of Lititz, Pennsylvania, even if it did boast having the first pretzel factory in America. I certainly wasn't going back to boring Liverpool, in upstate New

York, where my mom lived and I'd attempted a few semesters at Syracuse University before deciding college was a dead end for losers. I'd been desperately scanning Craigslist and other rental sites for the Big Apple with no luck.

I needed to find a place there. All professional actors should live in New York City if they're serious about pursuing a career in show business. And I was. I was destined for bigger things, I could just feel it.

I was going to be legendary.

Just then, the most unexpected thing happened. My archnemesis of all my castmates, Rebecca, sauntered into my room. All of us Ren Faire actors bunked together in a converted church that had been made into a dorm. I think my tiny room had once been a closet. Lots of people had bigger rooms, with two or three roommates. But I preferred being alone. Most people just irritated me with their stupid chatter. So I'd jumped on this small but private space when rooms were chosen the first day.

Rebecca was the one girl in the company who took every opportunity, at every turn this summer, to bust my game. The quintessential cock-blocker. She'd gossiped to other girls about my private nighttime maneuvers, dissuaded girls from hanging out with me, and made snide remarks about my lame abilities in the sack. That last thing had really burned me. Say what you wanted to about my fickleness, I was well-equipped and possessed a talented tongue. I'm not bragging, either. Lots of wenches had told me I was their best. I prided myself on never being a selfish lover. Girls always got their "cookies" first with me, and I often gave them multiples to enjoy during one of our sessions before I even had my first. So was it my fault if there were chicks who just assumed they were so awesome they'd make me want to hang around? Nope. Sorry, not sorry. It was hubris on their parts, I guess. Fidelity wasn't in my make-up. I never made any promises, so I never had any obligations. That's the way I rolled: no commitments.

But that didn't mean I didn't have goals, things I desired to possess, objectives I wanted to achieve. Like many seemingly unobtainable things, Rebecca intrigued me. Truth be told, her being a harpy, pain-in-the-ass bitch just made me lust for her all the more. I'd always liked gingers, too. Especially when the carpet matched the drapes. And now here she was, standing so close to my bed she could reach out and touch it.

"What's up Dan?" She leaned against my dresser and watched me as I zipped up my Pittsburgh Pirates duffle bag. I decided to play it cool, so I turned then kept my back to her and rolled up my jeans to pack, waiting for a few beats before answering.

"Not much, what's your deal?" I sat on my bed and looked her up and down. Maybe she'd been fighting an attraction to me all summer and that's why she'd been such a raging shrew. Maybe the whole thing about her warning other girls off of me was because she wanted me all to herself. I wondered if I should tell her, "Fear not, there's enough of the Dan-Man to go around." Probably she'd finally realized it was her last chance, so she was making her play for me. Her eyes looked hungry.

"I heard from Quentin that your plans for a place in New York fell through." She ran her finger up and down her neck.

Quentin was probably gloating to everyone who'd listen to his sorry ass. I wanted to tell him, Well, have at it, you cuckolded bastard. I know you found out I got a great hummer from your girlfriend Sara a couple of weeks ago in the church vestibule and that's why you're so pissed off. Idiot. But my attention could never stay on men like Quentin when I had a hot firecracker like Rebecca standing right in front of me. Her ice blue eyes twinkled. I'd never noticed how piercing they were.

"Yeah, well. Something will come up for me. It always does." I subtly drew my eyes down to my own crotch, hoping she'd get my powerful subliminal body language.

"Well, my roommate Carine is out of town for the next six weeks, and I was looking for someone to sublet her room…" She bit her juicy lower lip. Score another for the master.

"Now, that sounds like an offer I can't refuse," I smiled.

"I was hoping you'd say that," Rebecca grinned. She rarely did that. It made her even more beautiful. Softened her somehow. Maybe it drew attention away from her angular chin and her nose that was just a bit too large.

“My place is on the Upper West Side. Our roost is way up on the top floor, the twenty-ninth, so you can see the park from the balcony.”

I could see where that might appeal to some people, but I wasn’t so crazy about heights. Not that I was going to share that phobia with Rebecca. I didn’t want her to think anything about me was chickenshit in any way. So I just nodded.

"Does the building have a weight room?” I asked. “Not that it’s a deal-breaker but I do like to keep myself in shape…”

"Yes, I can see that.” She pursed her lips slightly. “It does. And the building also has a game room. If you like games…I love them.”

"Oh, I like games,” I smiled back, enjoying her innuendo. Often, having a bad relationship with someone at first made the sex that much hotter later. I was starting to really look forward to this.

"Great. I’m taking the train back tomorrow to get the place ready, to tie things up and stuff. Why don’t you hang out here for an extra day? I’ll see you there on Tuesday.”

"Sure,” I said. I had nothing to keep me here, but the Faire producers had announced we could stay here for a few days if we needed to. And I figured Rebecca needed to get herself ready. Maybe get a waxing, or something.

I doubted I’d be hanging around as long as she’d want me to, rooming with her for the whole six weeks. Banging the same chick for that long would get old no matter how good she was in the sack. I mean, there were only so many positions, right? But I knew having a place in the city while I searched for an apartment for the winter would make everything much easier.

The next day, I wasted time drinking in a local hole in the wall and whacked off twice thinking about Rebecca. Tuesday, I took a morning train out of downtown Lancaster to NY Penn Station. It was easy to find Rebecca's building, and since she'd given me a key and there was no doorman, I just made my way up to the twenty-ninth floor.

Even I, with my particularly kinky imagination, couldn't have begun to picture what awaited me inside. The living room was ordinary looking enough. In fact, it was so bland and impersonal, it looked like it had been ripped from the pages of an IKEA magazine. But I saw right away that the door to the bedroom in the back was slightly cracked. I also noticed that the apartment seemed only to be a one-bedroom versus the two-bedroom she'd claimed it was.

Oh, Rebecca, you must have wanted me so bad you resorted to a lie. I chuckled a bit to myself. Well, I wasn't about to disappoint her. It was nice to see there'd be no wasting time with some silly flirting and courting ritual. We'd just get right down to doing the nasty. Making the beast with two backs. That was just how I liked it.

"Anybody there?" I called out. From somewhere, music

softly played. “Free Bird” by Lynyrd Skynyrd. I was more of a Flo Rida and Pitbull fan myself, but I’d mash uglies to Celine Dion singing in the background if that’s what a bad kitty wanted.

"Why don’t you come in here?" I heard from the bedroom. I was happy to oblige.

When I opened the door, I felt like I’d stepped back in time. This room felt pre-Renaissance, more like the Middle Ages. There were whips, handcuffs, feathers, candelabras, and various potion bottles full of God-knows-what jewel-hued liquids. The walls of the room seemed to be covered in ancient tapestries. In the center was a large bed with a full canopy and ornate gold metal head and footboards. Through the translucent curtains, I could see what I assumed was Rebecca’s bare form.

"Wow, you are one sexy creature," I said parting the curtains. Rebecca was wearing a black Merry-Widow, her red hair cascading down her shoulders. She didn’t even look like the same uptight bitch from the Ren Faire who, when not in costume, always wore loose clothes and a tightly drawn pony-tail or bun. Her body was sinewy, and though she was a bit flat-chested, she had a tight ass complimented by long legs and a short, trim torso.

"Close the door, take off your clothes, and lie down," she ordered and stood up. Her eyes glinted as she nodded to the handcuffs and ankle cuffs attached to the top and bottom of the bed.

While I’ve always enjoyed a bit of light S&M, I’ve always

been the Dom. I wasn't sure how I'd like being the Sub. But because I was Rebecca's guest, I figured it was only polite to try this out. Besides, at that moment, I was as hard and pointy as the fake spear she had propped in the corner, so I wasn't about to risk her getting ticked off at me.

"Sure, whatever you want." I shucked off my clothes as quickly as I could and tried not to gloat when I noticed her taking in the magnificent view that was me. I positioned myself with my hands and feet spread and heard her click the handcuffs above my head and then watched her secure my ankle cuffs.

Then she did something odd. She laughed.

For a split second, I wondered if she knew what a boner-shrinker her laugh was. But then I didn't have time to wonder anything anymore. I was too busy screaming at the horror I was witnessing: Rebecca was sprouting wings and claws.

Her face stayed the same, but her body was turning into that of a monstrous bird. A giant vulture. Her laugh became a shrill cackle. She perched over me clearly enjoying my reaction. Then I stopped screaming and almost swallowed my own tongue when my mind finally processed what was happening.

She was a Siren. Not a sexy Disney-fied pretty fish lady. Not a mermaid. An authentic Siren. This was the real deal. Half-bird, half-woman. And very dangerous.

The bedroom contained an entity not from the European

Renaissance or from the Middle Ages but from the Greek Dark Age. I'd read tons of Greek mythology when I was younger 'cause I loved all the stories of the gods getting it on with each other and tricking unsuspecting mortals into sex. Zeus was my role model, my idol. But with all my fantasizing, I'd never expected to actually be in one of the stories.

"Go ahead, tell me to 'eat you,'" she taunted. "Or to 'swallow you whole,' or to 'suck it down like a good girl.'"

"No, please, no, just let me go..." I whimpered, and then I felt the warmth spread. How could I have...? I was so *not* turned on anymore. She still had her face, but she had a freakin' bird body! Then I realized, I'd just peed myself.

"We Sirens are still around because men like you give us reason to be. So, I guess I should be thanking you." Her lips stretched into a too-wide grimace covering most of her lower face. "So many monsters, hybrids, and even full gods have faded because they're irrelevant; nobody feeds energy into their purpose for being. But not us. Sirens are still going as strong as ever."

For a split second she seemed to be sad, I thought I had a chance, that maybe she was going to let me go with a harsh warning.

"I do especially miss the Kraken. But with no gods to require vengeance for perceived disrespect, no need exists for a Kraken." She scratched at the bed with her claws, shredding the sheets. "But it seems there are still many women who long for reprisal against a certain type of man." Then her face started to elongate, her nose and capacious mouth forming a beak. A beak that hovered over my liver, teasingly, before plunging into me.

Every morning I wake, alive again and whole, but still chained to this bed. And every evening, she comes again to rip me apart. I've been here so long that I've lost track of time.

It's the first long-term relationship I've ever had.

And, just as I suspected, it sucks.

Faces of Change

Jean Harkin

A girl at a Midwest university and a lion on the grasslands of Africa changed places. No one knows how this happened—or why.

After the switch, the red-haired girl looked as she always had, but her empowered soul was the lion's. She kept to herself, rarely speaking to people on campus; when she did, they found her difficult to understand. She often wandered to the prairie south of campus to walk barefoot, breathe the perfume of the prairie flowers, listen to whispers of the tall grass as the wind gushed through, and hear the calls of red-winged blackbirds.

The lion, with his kingly mane, appeared as usual but behaved oddly, according to the occasional lion who encountered him. With the soul of a girl, he had no wish to engage in battle with other lions. And he sought after his own prey, not wanting to depend on females of a pride to bring him food. The lion loved rolling in the tall grasses of the African savanna and gazing up at the deepest blue sky on the planet.

One hot day during the dry season, the lion lay down on a mattress of grass like fresh straw—still soft but firm. Eyes closed, the lion dreamed of playing on the veldt, chasing antelopes, and sniffing breezes to catch stories of fellow creatures.

Abruptly, he was kicked on his rump and awakened. Ready to fight on his feet, the instinct faded quickly when he saw the trouble surrounding him. A ring of men armed with guns targeted him. The tender soul within the lion looked up at the poachers. *Why must you hurt me? Do you not realize the great beauty of creation that I am? Please spare me.* As the men tightened their circle, the lion closed his eyes and mourned others of his tribe, fellow creatures suffering the misdeeds of heartless thugs, and wildlife in great numbers disappearing. The lion, realizing his hopeless position against a squadron of guns, aimed one more pleading look at the men and hoped for mercy.

The earth began to shake and vibrate. Blaring, trumpeting noises blasted the silent air of the savanna. The poachers turned their attention away from the lion and began hollering, tumbling over each other to escape the tumult of stampeding elephants rushing toward them. The poachers sprinted off in four directions.

With the danger suddenly past, the lion inhaled delicious earth scents once again. *I'm alive!* He stood up to welcome and thank the elephants for saving him. At the same time, he regretted his vulnerability and helplessness and inability to save himself.

That same day, the red-haired girl named Savannah walked away from the stately trees and college buildings at Iowa State and continued past campus town. Although it was February, with darkness falling fast on the afternoon, a deep urge to visit the prairie possessed her. As she left the campus farther and farther behind and clouds accelerated the arrival of nighttime, a chill formed around her shoulders. She shrugged it off and began to run, knowing her beloved prairie was near.

A mottled gray car spewing exhaust fumes pulled up alongside the roadway, blocking Savannah's path. The windows rolled down and out came hoots and whistles. "Hey girlie!"

Savannah loped around the car, slowed to a majestic walk, and kept her nose pointed straight ahead, down the country road toward her destination. No other cars or people were in sight. Her neck bristled, and her senses sharpened, alert for trouble.

Car doors opened and slammed shut. Four young men in dark jackets—two tall and lanky, two shorter and heftier—exited the car, rushed toward the lone girl, and surrounded her. This group was not from campus. *Danger!* One of the men grabbed her arm and began pulling her toward the ground.

Uh oh. They don't know who they've caught. Savannah called up the powers of her body, the strength of her lungs, and let out a tremendous roar, intense enough to frighten a herd of elephants. She flung off the weak arm that held hers, tossing the man into a ditch.

"My arm—it's broken!" he screamed. The others fell back in alarm as Savannah bared her teeth and charged at them, her red hair like a fiery war bonnet, and yellow eyes aflame. Her *tour de force* scattered the men and sent them scrambling back to the car, one of them still bellowing in pain. Savannah kept roaring to ensure their departure. The car's motor roared in return as it sped away.

Now for some peace and quiet. She watched the car's tail lights grow faint in the distance and then continued toward her rendezvous with the prairie.

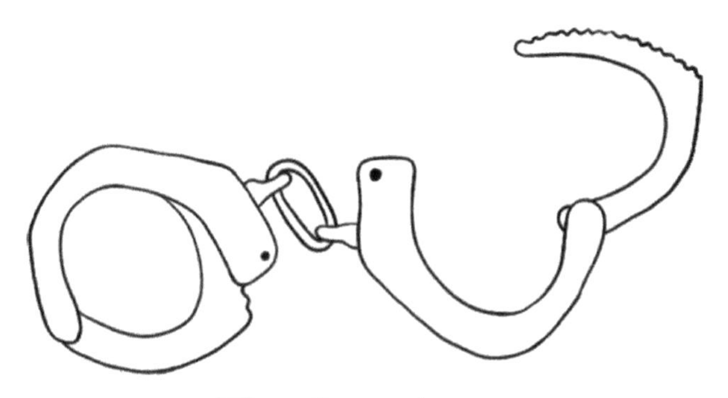

The Breakout

Laura Hazan

No one in Leonardtown wanted Cora convicted, but there she was, in the cell on my right. Cora cared for most of the babies in our part of the county. She'd been doing it for 50 years or more without any trouble. But several months ago, she turned her back from a bath for just a minute too long, and Janey Miller drowned.

Mr. Miller, both the local prosecutor and Janey's grandpappy, arrested Cora. Janey's parents saw it as a tragic accident, but Miller charged Cora anyway. A swift trial with a jury of his peers found her guilty, and the judge sentenced her to ten years with us in the women's county jail.

Rumor said Cora hadn't slept since the day of the accident. It seemed to be true. She prayed while she paced, only stopped to take some food, and never left her cell.

"Maybe we should encourage her to join us," I asked

the others one afternoon.

"Leave her be, Genie," Luscious McGee said. "She'll get tired soon enough."

Cora had no contact from the outside. Folks tried to see her in those first few weeks, but she refused to leave her cell. I didn't understand why she wouldn't want a visit; I delighted in every one.

I'd been trouble since the day I was born, came into this world breech, but not feet first like most breech babies. No, I came out butt first. My daddy said it's my best joke so far. He just loved that I mooned the old uppity doctor. I craved the thrill of daring deeds from that day forward. Harmless stuff like running naked out in the yard as a little tyke progressed to dangerous stuff like setting off fireworks during a basketball game. Then I turned to crime. Minor crimes, mind you, but there I was nonetheless: housed between an elderly black woman who drowned a baby and the local madame who didn't pay the sheriff enough for protection. I wonder if Cora remembered being at my birth; Daddy said she laughed louder than anyone.

* * *

Weeks passed, and Cora did not leave her cell. The rest of us gathered in the common area and played Crazy Eights or read magazines. Henry Adams, the morning guard, always brought us his wife's *Ladies' Home Journal* and *Life*.

"Cora must be resting when we're not looking," Little

Marie said as she shuffled the cards.

Little Marie, only four foot eleven, had a big habit of shoplifting. She mostly stole so her siblings could eat, but then she tried to steal a record player and a case of Elvis records from Kresge's.

"I think she goes to sleep after we do and wakes before us," Ally said when she looked up from her magazine. Ally kited checks. She didn't need the money; her daddy ran the largest crab packing factory in this part of the state. She just liked to steal—she and I shared that trait.

I picked up the cards Little Marie dealt. "Nope, neither of you is right. I've watched her closely. And she just don't, not the night I watched her anyway."

"Well if she don't stop that praying I'm liable to drown someone myself," Luscious McGee said.

Ally scowled. "You need to have some compassion, Luscious. Just like it suggests in this month's *Ladies' Home Journal*."

Luscious McGee slammed her cards on the table. "You can take that god damn magazine and…"

I reached over, picked up the cards and handed them back to her with a nod. I seemed the only one able to calm Luscious.

"What's she mumbling about over there all night?" Luscious asked.

"She's saying that she needs to get out of here and make it up to the baby. That she wants to pray over her grave, grieve with her momma, and care for her kin. It's the same thing over and over," I said.

"It's a mantra," the Beatnik said. The Beatnik's real name was Anne, but she didn't mind that we called her the Beatnik. On the outside, she wore a lot of black and read a lot of poetry. She also supplied little funny cigarettes to those in need. She said it wasn't right to charge for something that opened the mind, but they convicted her anyway. The Beatnik put a bookmark in her *New Yorker* and said, "It's what Buddhist monks say while meditating."

Henry, too old at sixty-five to still be a prison guard, walked in with a pot. "What are you chickens clucking about now?"

"Cora," I replied.

Henry shook his head. "You girls ought not mess with that one. She's upset a lot of important men in this town. No need getting involved."

"We feel badly for her, Henry. She didn't do no intentional harm," I said.

"And that's why she's here instead of the state pen. Though I wish she were. Some silly folk have started a protest out front. Pain in my ass." Henry put the pot down on the dining table. "Cooper's missus fixed a mighty nice oyster stew today. I'll see y'all tomorrow."

Jackson Cooper was only a few years younger than Henry. All the guards in our jail were close to retirement. We liked the old guys, and they liked us. Cooper's wife made our lunch every day except Sunday, and her meals were some of the best I'd ever tasted.

* * *

Several mornings later, I tried to coax Cora out of her cell. From outside her door, I told her, "Janey's in heaven now, and she wouldn't want you suffering for your mistake." I paused and got no response. "Janey's parents hadn't even wanted a trial—they're moving down the road to forgiveness."

Cora kept right on pacing and chanting. I decided to recite the name of every person I knew that Cora had cared for or helped bring into this world. After the first five names, she stopped praying but kept pacing. By now Little Marie and Ally stood behind me.

"Keep at it, Genie, she seems to be listening," Ally whispered.

I listed ten more names, and she stopped pacing. "Charles Monroe, my momma's second cousin. Betty Anne Monroe, his sister. Louisa Monroe, their baby sister." I pruned every branch of my family tree and then went to names of friends and neighbors. Cora finally sat down on her cot.

Little Marie clapped her hands like Cora just performed under the big top. "That's right, Cora, take a load off. Rest your eyes even, if they're feeling heavy."

Almost out of names, I signaled Ally to take over. She ran off and came back with some of the flowery stationary she saved for her beau and a fountain pen with scented ink. She wrote names, and I read them.

"Lloyd B. Wilson, Lydia B. Wilson, Lyle B. Wilson, Lauren B. Wilson..."

Cora put her feet up and then pulled her knees to her chest. She rocked back and forth in rhythm to my voice. "Patricia Hatcher, Eric Hatcher, Madeline Hatcher, Clare Hatcher, Karen James, John James..." I thanked God Ally had a large clan.

Little Marie grabbed some paper and a pen from my cell and wrote names too. I read from one list and then the other. Luscious McGee joined us. "Just lay back now, Cora. You need rest. We're here to take over, don't you fret no more about that baby."

"The baby." The first words Cora seemed to direct at us since she arrived. Then she started to sing a lullaby.

"Aloysius Richard..." I began, but before I could get the next two names out, Cora was back on her feet. I looked down at Ally's list and recited the next few names, but within minutes Cora stopped the song and started to pray again.

Luscious McGee yanked on my braid. "Damn it, Genie, keep going!"

"Why'd you bring up the baby?" I shouted back. "She seemed like she might actually lie down for some rest until you came over."

Ally and Little Marie tossed in their feelings, and the caterwauling followed.

Luscious pointed at us. "Stupid girls, why do you care what happens to some old nurse maid? Y'all act like she's the only decent person in the whole goddamned town."

"Enough!" Cora shouted above us. We'd been so absorbed in our own anger none of us noticed Cora step out of her cell. She started to pace again, but this time she directed her rant toward us. "Luscious McGee got one thing right; there ain't a decent person in this whole town. I kept bringing child after child into this world in hopes one of 'em would be good. God fearing. Responsible!" she shouted. "Baby Janey was supposed to be the last one, the one I was gonna stick with till I knew she was loving, respectable. I'm an old woman. I want to pass on knowing I done some good." She circled the common room dining table.

I tried to calm Cora before Henry heard. "You've done lots of good, Cora. But, you need to stop shouting before Henry comes in here. Why don't you sit down?"

"Henry Adams been mean to me since we was kids. Nothing he can do to me that ain't already been done. Those names, nearly every name you said has caused my heart to break. Not a decent person in the whole town."

I looked at the others; they'd all stepped back toward their cells. My mouth was dry and filled with regret. Cora had spittle on her chin and sweat on her brow. She reminded me of a traveling preacher I saw once; he shouted angry words from the pulpit yet promised goodness and hope with the Lord.

She stopped circling the table and pounded on it with both fists. "I need to get out of here. I need to make it up to the baby. I need to pray over her grave. I need to grieve with her momma. I need to care for her kin."

I walked nearer. "Cora, you need to calm down. You're going to break a hand."

The Beatnik came up next to me. "She's in a trance; she's not going to hear you. It's best to let her be."

"But she's going to hurt herself."

"She can't feel the pain. It's like the ancient Indian art of walking over hot coals. She's out of her body right now."

"Beatnik, you are so full of it," I finally replied.

With every sentence, Cora's hands started up near her face and ended down on the table. Her knuckles began to bleed.

Henry walked in with a tray of tableware in preparation for lunch. "What in blue blazes is going on in here?" Henry shouted over Cora's mantra. "Cora, quit punching that table." He moved toward her.

"I wouldn't go near her, Henry," The Beatnik warned. "She is not herself."

Henry paid no mind. "Go back to your cell, both of you, and stay there." He put the tray down. "Cooper will be here any minute, Cora, with a nice hot meal. Let's just sit down and wait for him, quietly." He put his hand on her left forearm.

Without hesitation, she grabbed him and pulled him into a headlock. A powerful woman with a half foot advantage over Henry, he could not fend her off. She grabbed a butter knife from the tray and held it up to his throat. Those knives didn't cut through boiled potatoes, but in Cora's strong hand it was sharper than a tanner's blade.

Luscious McGee ran over to the table. "Cora, you're not in your right mind."

"Luscious McGee," Cora replied as if on an afternoon stroll, "You've always talked more than anyone I know. I'm getting out of here. I need to make it up to the baby. I'm going to pray over her grave. I'm going to grieve with her momma. I'm going to care for her kin. Henry's going to help me get out of here. Maybe you should too."

"Cora, no one's going anywhere," Luscious McGee said. Ally, Little Marie, the Beatnik, and I gathered behind Luscious.

Little Marie jumped up and down behind me. "What's she saying? I can't see. What's she doing now?"

"She's just stopped," I replied. "Quit jumping on me. She says we need to go with her."

"I'm not up to a jailbreak," Little Marie replied. "That's too dangerous."

Luscious McGee turned to us. "Will you all hush! No one's leaving this jail."

The Beatnik grinned. "She's already gone. 'My prison walls cannot control/The flight, the freedom of the soul.' I'm going with her."

I didn't understand half of what The Beatnik usually said, but this time she made sense. "Me too."

Ally nodded. "I'm in."

The three of us linked arms and pushed past Little Marie and Luscious McGee. Cora kept repeating, "I'm getting out of here. Henry's helping me get out of here." Then, clear as day, she said something I'll never forget. "I need a gun." She looked around and walked over to the desk, pulled Henry along with her.

"Cora, a gun's a very bad idea, very bad. You're going to do hard time for this," Luscious said. "You girls need to get back."

I took two steps back, but Ally and The Beatnik held firm. "She ain't leaving alone," I replied as I stepped back in line.

Cora put down the knife and grabbed a handgun from a holster slung over the back of the desk chair. She pointed the gun at Henry's head. "Okay, Henry, we're going outside now."

Henry squirmed. "Cora, please just leave me be. Go out the door, I don't care, but leave me here."

I heard Little Marie start to cry. Luscious stepped in front of the door to the outside. The Beatnik, Ally, and I drew closer together and got right behind Cora and Henry.

"Luscious McGee, you best move out of the way. I don't plan on hurting no one, but I won't let you get in my way neither," Cora said as she got almost nose to nose with Luscious.

"This is craziness Cora," Luscious replied. I saw her

wrinkle her nose as the bitter odor of fear invaded the space. Luscious waved, "Come over here, Little Marie. You and I are the only sane people in this place right now, so we best go with them to make sure no one gets hurt."

Little Marie stood next to Luscious but kept on crying. She whispered something to Luscious, who put her arm around Little Marie and said to the room, "I've been around long enough to know best. I'm going to open the door and walk out with Little Marie. Then I want the three stooges over there to join us. You come out with Henry, and we'll circle up around you. That should prevent you from trying to shoot Henry, in thoughts of hitting one of us, and prevent the police from shooting you."

"You ain't in charge here, Luscious McGee. This is my escape," Cora replied.

Luscious McGee took her arm from round Little Marie's shoulders and crossed it with her other over her ample bosom. "You ain't got no choice right now, Cora. You do it my way, or you go through me."

I thought back to the easy comfort of the common area and cursed myself for ever starting this.

Cora shifted from one foot and then the other. "Fine, we can do it your way. Go on, then. Open the door."

* * *

One by one, we stepped out into the glare. It was quiet in the parking lot, only the crunch of the oyster shells underfoot accompanied our escape. Cora and Henry came out of the building last, and we formed a human chain around them just as Luscious described. I held hands with the Beatnik and Ally, Little Marie took Ally's hand on her other side, and Luscious closed the circle once Cora and Henry entered. We inched our way across the small parking lot until we reached the main road.

A quarter mile down, we passed the protesters. Three college students from Baltimore and Mrs. Meriwether erected "Free Cora" signs just down from the main gates of the old jail on the road to town.

Mrs. Meriwether ran up next to us. "Y'all supposed to be locked up?"

"We just going to visit with Janey's momma," Cora replied.

Mrs. Meriwether straightened her hat and smiled. "Well, I'll be damned. You girls got her out."

The Beatnik grinned too. "She got herself out, we're just assisting."

"I'm gonna make a new sign and walk along with y'all if you don't mind."

"Suit yourself," Cora said.

Within five minutes, Mrs. Meriwether and the college students marched behind us and sang "Let My People Go." The Beatnik sang along.

We saw Cooper's truck on the horizon. "Thank the Lord," Henry muttered.

Little Marie howled, "I don't want to die!"

"We're not going to die," I said. "Everyone just keep walking."

Cooper pulled up beside us in his rusty pickup. "You girls ain't supposed to be out for a stroll. Just turn yourselves around now and no one will get in trouble."

"Can't do that," Cora said. "I'm going to grieve with the baby's momma."

"Cora, you need to let Henry go now!" Cooper shouted through the cloud of dust we created.

"Going to see Baby Janey's momma. Henry's helping me," Cora shouted back.

Several police cars greeted us at the foot of Main Street. Cooper stopped his truck and joined behind us, rifle in hand. As we crested the first rise of the hilly street, I heard a cheer go out. Dozens of townsfolk lined the busy thoroughfare, and we each smiled at the encouragement. Even Little Marie managed a smirk.

Cora looked left and right at the many faces gathered to watch her escape. Then she pulled the gun from Henry's temple and fired a shot between Ally and me into the crowd. A body hit the ground.

"Damn, Cora, this is a peaceful break!" I shouted.

Cora moved the gun back to the indentation on Henry's head. "Jimmy Russell. Beats his wife. Why isn't he in jail?"

We all knew she was right, and apparently so did the rest of the town. No one rushed us, and no one moved to help him. They just stepped over him and started to follow us. It made me think of that disturbing story "The Lottery" The Beatnik read to us from her *New Yorker* some months back.

"What's with these people?" Luscious McGee asked.

Then *BANG!* "William Tyler—pesters children," Cora said.

Cora continued to dispense justice the entire half mile up the hill. In less than three blocks, she shot five people. Every one known for the crimes they committed but for which they were never punished.

We finally stopped in front of Baby Janey's house. The front door was closed, the shades were drawn, and faded black bunting still hung from the porch rails. Luscious McGee broke the circle, and Cora stepped out of the halo of protection. She released Henry, handed me the gun, and started up the porch steps.

She turned to us as she reached the top step and said, "I believe justice has been served today. You ladies better head on back to jail. I'm going to rest now while I wait for Janey's momma to join me."

Cora walked over to one of the ladder-backed rockers on Janey's porch and sat down. She closed her eyes and started humming a lullaby. Within minutes she was sound asleep. Rumor has it she never woke.

Blaise

Lori Ubell

She looked like a stone butch, but it wasn't that simple. She was a twisted girl who could only come with her clients, none of whom were female.

Not that her lovers minded. She could certainly make them come. And she was so handsome, with eyes the color of a ripe bruise, and a smile that made you hot from your neck down to the tips of your toes.

And strong. So strong she could split a log with one blow. So strong that if she held you down, you couldn't get up, no matter how fit you thought you were.

She preferred girls from the upper middle class, and she never let them whore.

"You couldn't stand it, not for one day," she'd say, as she packed that little bag with the red silk underwear she never wore at home. Then she'd be gone, for a night or a week, coming back exhausted and more silent than usual.

After a long bath, she'd emerge and dig a wad of cash

out of the bag.

"Here, darlin'," she'd say, tossing it on the bed, "for you." She wouldn't talk about what she'd done for it, but the girl always knew.

And sometimes, in bed, she'd imitate the men, and they'd both laugh so hard that life seemed good, at least in that moment.

But the rages came without warning, and they were terrifying.

At first, you'd just hear about them.

Late one night, she threw her bicycle through a plate glass window downtown. No one saw, but it made the 11 o'clock news. It was in the days of the Weather Underground and Baader-Meinhof, and the newscaster speculated about what it could mean.

What it meant was that Blaise's bike had a flat, and she was walking it home when a guy started hassling her.

"Hey, what are you, a boy or a girl? Hey, bull dyke, wanna fight? Hey, chickie, wanna play?"

He was young and not especially big. Blaise knew she could take him, but she didn't want to fight, not downtown at 2:00 a.m., so she kept walking.

When he said, "Just give me the bike, and I'll leave you alone," she turned around and spat in his face.

"You bitch!" he screamed, and grabbed the back wheel. Blaise was quick in those days, and she yanked it away, heaving it through the window of a men's haberdashery.

Alarms went off, and she and the guy ran in opposite

directions.

"But now you have no bike," said the girlfriend, looking up at her with big brown eyes. "How will you get around?"

Blaise shrugged.

"You can buy me one, can't you?"

The girl could, and did. Not with Blaise's money, because that money always disappeared, spent on dinners out, and pounds of pot, and the occasional rock concert. But the girl, a student, had a large allowance from parents far away. So Blaise got a new bike, and no one ever knew what happened to the window downtown.

That girl didn't last, and neither did the next. It got colder, and Blaise got more desperate. By the time I met her, her smile almost never showed.

I was in a reckless mood, wearing dress and heels to the bar in a time when the normal garb, both butch and femme, was jeans and a flannel shirt. I was tired of that, and tired of going home alone.

"I've heard about you," I whispered in her ear as I linked my arm through hers.

She looked down at me, eyes glittering with lust and narcotics.

"What have you heard?"

"That you're the best fuck in town."

And plenty more, but it seemed irrelevant.

"What do you want to do about it?"

I dragged her home, and she stayed.

For weeks, all we did was laugh and fuck, eating Popeye's chicken when we got hungry. I didn't answer the phone, and the only mail I opened was the unemployment check.

One day, she said, "I have to work tonight."

I knew what she meant, but I made her tell me. I could always get her to tell me things.

So she went to work, coming home the next day at noon with swollen lips and a dark scowl.

When she'd cleaned herself, she said, "Let's go out to eat." And over dinner, she told me the story of her life. How her step-father had raped her, and her mother had thrown her out, saying, "Why don't you tie a bed to your back?"

It sounded grim, but it was the sixties, and Venice Beach was filled with runaways and throwaways. She learned to steal. She learned to whore. She bought herself some roller-skates, and skated up and down the boardwalk, plying her trade. Some bad things happened, but she shrugged them off and went on. What else could she do?

"Why didn't you stay down there?" I asked.

"My mom's up here," she said. I blinked. I couldn't believe she wanted to be anywhere near that woman.

None of her friends knew her real name, or that she had a mother who lived on Skid Row in an SRO, or a sister in foster care somewhere in California, but I did. I even met the mother, who said to me, "Better keep Sherine around at least 'til spring, so she can keep chopping your wood."

When the bill for this knowledge came due, I nearly couldn't pay it.

It was 3:00 a.m., and Blaise had been gone two days. I woke up to a knife at my throat. She wore a stocking over her face, and I didn't know it was her until after she'd bound me and made me cry out against my will.

I forgave her, but for her it was over, and she moved on. The next girl got beaten so badly she ended up in the hospital. I lost track of her after that.

Years later, when that Dire Straits song came out, you could almost believe it was about her. The only movie she ever made, though, wasn't on location, but in a crappy motel at the edge of town. If that 8mm still exists, it shows, in grainy black and white, a girl being gang-raped. And if the cameraman happened to zoom in on her face, he captured the last time tears ever fell from those long-dead eyes.

All Is Revealed

Chloe Hagerman

The first thing I'm aware of is that I'm still in my pajamas. I can feel goosebumps prickling up my arms and legs, and a shudder tears through my body. I can feel a rough carpet under my bare feet. It's worn out and slightly sticky, something that I probably would not choose to be walking on barefoot if I had the choice. That's when it hits me: I'm not in my room. My bedroom is hardwood without any rugs or carpeting.

At this moment, my surroundings become visible to me, as if they were waiting for me to come to this realization. I'm standing at the beginning of a long hall, surrounded on both sides by towering bookshelves. The dark red carpet stretches out into darkness. Turning around, I see a wall of books behind me, preventing me from going back. I crane my neck to look up. I'm just an inch under six feet, but even so it looks like it would take at least three of me standing on each other's shoulders to reach the books at the very top. Above the shelves, green stained-glass lamps are throwing an eerie light, but beyond that there is only blackness. I can't see the ceiling; I can't even tell what the lamps are suspended from. They might be floating, for all I know. They probably are. Nothing needs to make sense. This is obviously a dream, after all.

I've had dreams before—who hasn't?—but I've never been certain they were dreams until my eyes open in the morning. I've never had a dream that took me to a fantastical world or allowed me to do improbable things. As boring as that sounds, my dreams have always had at least a foot and a half firmly planted in reality. I've had nightmares that caused me to wake up in a sweat in the middle of the night, but they are something along the lines of being held at gunpoint on a street in my hometown. I was never chased or devoured by ghosts or monsters.

So I had no reason to question my surroundings until I woke up to the glow-in-the-dark stars on my ceiling. That was until this...library. It doesn't remind me of any library I've ever seen before, but I can easily see where I might have gotten inspiration from real life to amalgamate into this place. This is definitely the first time I can say, *Okay, you're clearly dreaming. Now the question is what are you going to do about it?*

The first thought that comes to my head is of a book I read years ago in college. *Journey to Ixtlan*. The writer is studying under a shaman, who presents him with the challenge of learning to control his dreams. The first test is to look down at his hand during a dream. Instinctively, I do the same. I look down at my right hand, seeing my silver thumb ring and the blue woven friendship bracelet around my wrist. My skin is red and cracked; I haven't been putting on moisturizing lotion as regularly as I should. But my hand doesn't hurt at all. Of course, it wouldn't in a dream. Okay. So I looked at my hand. That was easy. I'll be a regular Dream Master in no time.

I set myself my own challenge: take a step. I raise my foot and place it down again as easily as if I was walking in the real world. The carpet where I've put my foot down doesn't feel as sticky now. I look down at where I was standing before and see that that small section of the rug, right back near the end of the aisle, is so worn down I can almost see the floor through it. How long have I been standing there?

Slowly, cautiously, I take a few more steps, and then my stride becomes longer and more confident. But the horizon isn't changing. Out of the blackness comes only more shelves. The carpet stretches out in front of me like a long tongue, and I can't see where it goes. I can't tell if I'm headed into or out of the maw.

I start jogging, but more of the same just keeps coming at me, on and on and on. I get more and more confused. Am I supposed to take this as a metaphor for my life or something? Is this supposed to give me insight into the human condition? We keep moving, keep running, and end up going nowhere? Wow. Deep. This is becoming the first dream that could actually do me in with boredom before anything else. At least if there was someone else to talk to, it might be more interesting here.

After what feels like at least a few minutes of walking, I pause and take a closer look at some of the books on the shelves around me. There're some titles in English that I can read, such as *Jack the Ripper Revealed* or *Complete Chronology of the Battle of Bunker Hill*, but others are in strange symbols or in languages I can't understand. What strikes me, however, is that all of the volumes appear to be in excellent condition. There's no sign of wear on the spines, no threads out of place on the woven covers. There's no layer of dust to take away from any of the colors or even a scent of dust in the air. In fact, there's no smell at all. The books don't smell like they're new, and yet they are immaculate. I tip one book halfway out of its place on the shelf and examine the pages. No sign of dog ears or tears. As lonely as this library is, it's definitely got the best quality control of any I've ever seen.

However, I'd much rather have some company, all things being equal. Staring at the hallway stretching before me, still ending in darkness, I yell, "Hello?" My voice resonates in the air around me, traveling away until it is swallowed up into the black air. No response. Slightly irritated now, I begin walking. As soon as I take another step, the scenery in front of me changes. I can see a larger room up ahead. Unable to help myself, I break into a run until I am there, halting just at the edge.

It's a circular room lined with bookshelves like the ones in the hall behind me, with a large crystal chandelier hovering over everything. There are tables surrounded by plush brown armchairs, sporting amber lamps. But, most importantly, across the room from me I can see someone taking books off the shelves. It's an older, gray-haired man in a green sweater and khaki pants. I weave my way through the tables and call out, "It's so good to see someone here."

The man turns around. He's got a huge stack of books of various sizes in his hands and is wearing glasses with thick lenses. As soon as he sees me, his mouth turns down at the corners, his lip trembles, and his eyes go extra shiny. He looks like he's about to cry. I stop dead in my tracks, staring back at him.

"Welcome to the library," he says. I can hear the tears in his voice even if they haven't fallen from his eyes yet.

Instinctively, I cross my arms over my chest. I've only got a thin, pink silk top and blue short shorts on. Hardly conventional library attire. But his eyes never leave my face. My clothes couldn't matter less to him; all I know is that he wishes I weren't here. This is quickly becoming the oddest dream I've ever had. But I don't want to stay in this position forever before I wake up, so I ask, "Can I read any of these books?"

The man sniffs and nods. "Yes. Anything here is open to you. Most people your age prefer to start off in the video section." He points to a hallway off to his right, which again heads off into blackness. "Enjoy your stay," he says before turning back to the shelves.

I turn in the direction he is pointing and start heading off. *Am I really going to spend the rest of this dream watching a movie?* I shake my head at the idea. As I leave the circular section and the librarian behind, I don't know how long this walk is going to take, so I start running through tomorrow's activities in my head. My little sister and I are taking care of our parents' house while they're off on a long cruise, and they're due back in just a few days. We need to get the house cleaned and the garden weeded before they get back. Our parents are avid gardeners, so the outdoor tasks are definitely going to be more time-consuming. Maybe I can foist that off on my sister by convincing her the house will be harder…I can do a quick dusting over every room and pull out the vacuum cleaner…maybe get the floors mopped too, if I really feel like going the extra mile…

This mental checklist must have taken up more time than I realized, because the next thing I know I'm glancing at a shelf and seeing that the books have been replaced by plastic DVD cases. They look just as clean and new as the covers of the books did. I stop and take a look at the titles. *Jimmy Hoffa's Grave Revealed. Amelia Earhart's Disappearance Revealed. Zodiac Killer Revealed.* I remember seeing similar titles on some of the books back in the original hallway. This gives me pause. 'Revealed?' What is this, some kind of trashy conspiracy theory collection? My opinion of this library's quality is plummeting.

Rolling my eyes, I continue forward and come upon a space that looks like a video section in a regular library. Monitors are placed on long desks, and big black dividers are placed between them, allowing viewers some privacy. There are, in fact, a few other people here with me, but they are all wearing headphones and staring enraptured at their TV sets.

One boy who looks like he's still in middle school is watching his video with wide, round eyes. An older woman has tears rolling down her eyes as she stares at her screen. I take a quick glance over her shoulder and see that she is watching two large airplanes collide on an airport runway. The impact and ensuing fireball make me shudder and shrink away. I decide not to disturb her and browse one of the surrounding shelves. I see more and more titles about something or other being revealed and think that I'm in this library's crazy idea of a history section. I've never been much of a history buff, so I decide to see if I can find a section on current events. In the middle of one shelf, a title catches my eye. *Crescent City Killer Revealed.* This gives me pause. Crescent City is where my family lives.

I take the DVD off the shelf and turn it over to see if there's any more information on the back. Nothing. No dates or anything. This might just be something like a soap opera or propaganda of some sort. Then an idea hits me. What if it's not? Older stuff like Jack the Ripper and Amelia Earhart are glimpses into the past. Maybe this is a glimpse into the future? If it is, and I watch this video and learn the killer's identity before he strikes, I might be able to save someone's life. I could save multiple lives. The idea excites me so much that I start to shake a little bit. I can watch this video and learn this sicko's identity, and when I wake up in the morning I can go to the police and stop him before he has a chance to get started. Yes. I have to watch this.

I turn around and see that there is an available monitor right behind me. Plopping down on the chair, I pop the DVD into the tray and slip a pair of headphones over my ears. They are very comfortable, and they completely block out every sound except the faint buzz from the TV. No wonder everyone else in here was so fixated on what they were seeing on the screen; it's like these headphones shut out the rest of the world.

I take a quick glance both ways to see if anyone is watching me, and when I see that no one is, I prop my feet up on the desk. *Concentrate,* I tell myself as the screen boots up. *Study everything closely. You're going to get this guy.*

The movie—or documentary, whatever it is—doesn't bother with opening credits or a title or anything. It just goes right into the action. There's a tall man dressed in black creeping through a dark house in the middle of the night. I study his face. Short brown hair; long nose; a mole on his left cheek. I don't recognize him. His hands are covered with purple latex gloves. The small knife in his right hand glints menacingly as he turns. It looks just slightly smaller than a switchblade. He finds the staircase to the second floor and starts ascending. He goes slowly and carefully, testing each individual step, checking for the possibility of a loud creak. Every so often, he will glance back over his shoulder, and then focus on the climb in front of him again.

Okay, if you don't know this guy, study the house. Maybe you'll recognize the place and you can warn whoever's inside.

He pauses to observe a picture on the wall near the top of the staircase, and even in the dim light of the video I notice something that gives me pause.

I remove my legs from the table so that I can lean forward and study the images better. The figures in the picture look eerily familiar. Peering closer, I stop breathing as I recognize one of my family's portraits from years ago. My parents, my sister, and I are all sitting on the floor around our old dog, a bloodhound named Westin who died five years ago. I may not recognize the killer, but I recognize the house all too well.

Calm down, I tell myself. *Remember, this is the future you're looking at. Your dream is giving you a chance to catch this guy. Look at him again.* I peer closely at his face. I still don't think I've ever seen him before, but maybe he's someone my parents know. I can try calling or emailing them when I get up in the morning. If they give me something to go on, then I can take the information to the police.

Now the man is creeping down the upstairs hallway. He stops at the first door on the right and slowly edges it open, again not wanting to run the risk of a creak. I suck in my breath as I realize which room he's going into.

The windows are open in the bedroom. A fan buzzes in the corner. It's a hot summer night, so I'm sprawled out on the bed. The covers are thrown back, and there's a white sheet tangled around my legs. My head is turned to the wall away from the door, and my hair is covering my face.

The man pauses over my bed, staring silently down at me. I concentrate as hard as I can, trying to pull something from this video that will give me a name or a place I might have seen this guy before. He's looking down at me like he knows me. Or it could just be association with my family. Then I notice something else that gives me pause: the clothes I am wearing. Pink silk top. Blue short shorts. I glance down at my lap, take in my familiar clothes, and a cold wave of doubt starts to gnaw at me.

Did I leave the windows open in my room before I went to sleep tonight? I know I turned the fan on. The sound of it running created a kind of white noise that helped me drift off. But did I open the windows? I can't remember. But this is still the future…it has to be.

Slowly, ever so slowly, the man reaches out his left hand and tilts my head to stare up at the ceiling. There's not a flinch or so much as a tick from my face; I'm completely out, sleeping much more soundly than I usually do when it's hot. I'm torn right now. Part of me is wishing desperately that I could wake up this instant just to make sure I'm all right, but the other half of me thinks that if I were to do that, this man standing over me with a knife is exactly what I would see.

The man has been so slow and methodical up until this moment that I almost miss his next actions. I wish that I had.

He clamps his left hand over my mouth, and with his right hand, he brings the blade across my throat.

I clap both hands over my mouth to hold back my scream. I fancy I can feel a light line drawn across my neck, almost like a tickle. My hands go to my throat, expecting to feel the cut, expecting to feel hot, slimy blood cascading down my chest. Instead, I just feel my own clammy hands. Did that really just happen? *No, this is the future. You wear those pajamas all the time in the summer. Keep concentrating. Look for clues.*

Then I remember the titles of all the DVDs and books I saw. *Jack the Ripper Revealed. Amelia Earhart Revealed.* "Revealed." Answers to questions no one was able to answer in life. If this killer is "revealed"...does that mean that nobody ever catches him?

It takes me a second to realize that the film is still going. The man has now left my body behind without a second thought and is making his way back into the hallway.

There is another door directly across from him.

"No," I croak. After seeing my own throat cut, I'm amazed that I still have a voice. But it's still there, and it's rapidly gaining steam. This nagging doubt in my mind is getting stronger by the second. I lean forward until my nose is practically touching the TV screen. "No, no, no. No."

The Crescent City Killer edges the other door open just as slowly and cautiously as he did mine. He creeps into the second bedroom. The bed he approaches is smaller—just a single—against the far wall. There, lying prone under a canopy of sheets with stars and galaxies printed on them, is my little sister. Much as he did with me, the killer stands over her for a few moments, staring down at her, undoubtedly relishing what he's about to do.

"No, no, no! Wake up! Wake up! Get out of there!" I'm yelling.

He plants his left hand over her mouth, raises the knife—

"NO—!"

A hand clamps down on my shoulder, making me jump. I spin around and gasp in horror and despair as I stare up into my sister's confused face.

Pack Mentality

Sydney Culpepper

The flier screamed in tall red letters, "END THE OPPRESSION—HUMANOIDS ARE PEOPLE TOO!"

Anita's mouth turned down in a frown as she retracted her hand from the can of *frijoles*. She sighed and tried again, reaching for the can behind the first one, but it too had one of the rally fliers taped to the front of it. A quick scan revealed that all the other cans had square fliers taped to them as well. She turned and retreated down the aisle to leave the store, too annoyed to simply pull off a flier and buy the beans.

She made her way to the front of the store, pushing her way past a vampire with a basket full of vamp-grade sunscreen and vegan blood packets. She turned the collar of her jacket up against the biting autumn wind that greeted her as she walked out of the automatic doors. Flares of annoyance shot up inside her as she crossed through the parking lot to the busy street the store faced.

All she'd wanted to do was take a simple trip down the street to the local Weremart (*The One Stop Shop For All Your Super Natural Needs!*) to pick up some ingredients for dinner, but she couldn't even manage that without running into more propaganda.

The mythic-humanoids' rights movement had really picked up speed these past few months ever since Senator Cordelia Irving came out as a selkie. Every news outlet covered the scandal for weeks afterward. Despite calls for her resignation from the conservatives, Senator Irving began actively backing the then feeble movement. In an effort to seem 'in with the times,' other politicians also joined the movement. This unprecedented amount of support for humanoids had been spurring rallies and marches to pop up all over the country, much like the one that was being advertised all over every inch of this city—including the cans of beans.

Anita's feelings toward the movement were conflicted for a number of reasons. The first was that she wasn't particularly fond of humanoids seeing as her family was murdered by a werewolf when she was six. Another reason was that the rational side of her recognized that most humanoids weren't violent in nature and just wanted to have basic rights. Like elves, for instance. Most of them either wanted to live in the woods and be left alone, or they wanted to open eclectic jewelry and clothing shops.

It was the dangerous humanoids that gave her caution,

such as vampires, werewolves, and shape shifters. Most of the oppressive laws that were currently in existence had been created to keep the general human population safe. Still, many of the laws were unfair and invasive. Anita was sympathetic to the humanoids that resisted their violent nature, but, at the same time, she knew firsthand how monstrous they could be. She was, after all, a werewolf herself.

Anita joined the crowd that stood at the street corner waiting for the lights to change. The cold air bit at her nose and burned her throat whenever she breathed in. She could feel the wolf inside her as it shivered and curled its tail more tightly around itself. Then, it perked its ears and sniffed. Anita's stomach grumbled as the smell of a hot dog cart three blocks up and two blocks right reached her nose. She thought back to the beans she didn't buy and sighed.

The lights turned, the traffic stopped, and she moved forward with the rest of the crowd.

Her being a werewolf added yet another layer of complication to her feelings about the movement. The werewolf that had killed her father, mother, and older brother had also tried to kill her, clawing her chest so deeply she had almost died. Instead, though, she was turned into a werewolf and bore the scars from the attack on her chest like a sigil. Thus, having been a werewolf from the age of six, Anita had spent nearly her entire life being the subject of ridicule and hatred

All humanoids had to register their 'condition' with the government so they could be tracked in the humanoid database and so proper precautions could be made. In Anita's case, this meant daily dosages of the wolfsbane elixir that would keep the wolf inside her dormant. For all humanoids, it meant that anyone they worked with—teachers, bosses, landlords—had to be informed of their condition, or the humanoid would face legal consequences and charges of malintent. This ensured that everyone saw Anita first as a wolf, not a girl, and they'd never see her as anything else.

As a child, Anita was bullied often for being a werewolf. Every year her identity was announced to the class so other students could "keep themselves safe," and it always ostracized her from anyone who could have been her friend if she hadn't been a werewolf. Kids were cruel and called her "beast" and "wolfie," and she was always picked last for teams. She'd been beaten up on countless occasions, and not a single person had done anything to help her, not even her grandfather, who'd taken her in after the attack and raised her. He especially resented her for being a werewolf. She often thought that it stemmed from his hatred of the werewolf who had turned her, the one who had killed his only daughter.

Anita and her grandfather had to move almost every year due to her being a werewolf. The bullying inevitably reached a high point, and she and her grandfather were forced to move cities again. The reasons varied—a student would claim Anita threatened to bite them, parents would stage a protest against Anita's presence in school, a teacher would fail her on purpose—but the result was always the same. Finally, though, she graduated high school and moved to this city for a fresh start, but life didn't get better from there. It was hard to find anywhere that would hire a werewolf, and even harder to find a place that would keep her on longer than a few weeks. She endured glares and shifty looks and sometimes abuse from her neighbors, and she had to accept that there was nothing she could do about the fact that her landlord owned a gun loaded with the fatal silver bullets, and that he carried it whenever he had to interact with her. Still, she'd been here for nearly two years, which was the longest she'd ever stayed in one place since before the attack.

One would think that fellow humanoids would find support in each other, but that wasn't the case. She certainly hadn't been the only humanoid in the many schools she'd gone to as a child and a teenager, but humanoids that associated with each other were met with even more suspicion and hatred than lone humanoids. The most support they ever gave each other was perhaps a passing glance in the hall, and sometimes the understanding in the other humanoid's eyes would be enough to get her through the day. It made her feel like she perhaps wasn't as alone as she thought.

That isolation, however, was beginning to change.

Now, humanoids stood together as a single group, not various races or individuals. It didn't matter anymore if they were vampires, dwarves, elves, or centaurs. They were united under oppression, which was ironically one of the things the humans had been trying to prevent with the tyrannical laws.

The wolf pricked its ears, and Anita lifted her eyes at the sound of people shouting up ahead of her. She saw a small group of people with signs and fliers that were advertising the rally that was taking place tomorrow. Senator Irving's face was plastered on several signs, and one announced that she was going to be the keynote speaker at the rally.

"Help us fight for our rights!" she heard one of the activists shout. "Come to our rally tomorrow night!"

"Go to hell!" a man yelled from across the street.

Anita slowed as she approached the group of activists. She really didn't want to deal with more propaganda, but her apartment was just a couple blocks further, and she didn't want to take the long way around. With a resigned sigh, she moved forward and hunched her shoulders, hoping she gave off a "Don't bother me!" vibe.

Apparently, she didn't.

"Humanoids have the same wants and needs as humans do," a girl said, stepping directly into Anita's path. "Job security, insurance, marriage—help us fight for our rights!"

The fliers clutched in her hand declared, "WE

DESERVE EQUALITY!"

Anita's insides twisted uncomfortably, and she was about to offer a halfhearted excuse when the girl sniffed the crisp air and leaned in close to Anita.

"You might want to stay more hydrated," she whispered, her eyes knowing and kind.

Anita cringed in shame and embarrassment at the all-too-familiar euphemism. The girl must be werewolf too if she could pick up on Anita's wolf scent. Normally, her scent was suppressed by the elixir, but recently the drink had started wearing off sooner and sooner despite her taking the same dosage she had been for the past fourteen years. Not only did it mean that she was more susceptible to the wolf inside her, but government officials often performed surprise blood tests on registered werewolves to make sure they were taking their wolfsbane, and if she was caught with not enough elixir in her system…

"Thanks," Anita mumbled, starting to move past.

"Wait," the girl said, pinching Anita's jacket sleeve. "If you're alone, my friends and I have this place downtown. You could come by if you wanted."

The girl's smile was gentle, and it broke Anita's heart. She was extending an offer for Anita to join her pack. It wasn't an official pack, of course, probably just a group of friends. Still, the wolf pined for the companionship that a pack offered, but Anita couldn't let it happen. There was a dark, secret part of her that wanted to accept the wolf and be part of a pack, but she was too afraid of what could happen if she did, too afraid of the wolf.

"I can't, sorry," Anita said, tugging her jacket out of the girl's grip. She shouldered past the other activists and half-jogged down the sidewalk before darting into the closest alley.

Anita unzipped her jacket and reached into the inside pocket, pulling out a slim flask. Her nose wrinkled in distaste as she unscrewed the lid. The liquid inside was a deep violet color, and though it had no smell, she knew the taste was intensely bitter. It was the wolfsbane elixir she drank every day. Aconite, more commonly known as wolfsbane, was fatally toxic to everyone except werewolves, but on werewolves it still had an incredibly negative effect. If taken in too high a dosage, it could kill the werewolf. Anita took just enough to keep herself human, but it always left her feeling nauseous and tired, and had her mouth and throat tingling for hours.

Unlike the stories people told decades ago, when creatures and humanoids were still thought of as myths and legends before modern technology made it impossible to hide, werewolves didn't only transform on the full moon. The urge to transform was much stronger during the full moon, for unknown yet probably magical reasons, but it could be resisted with the help of wolfsbane or with years of practiced control. But even with control, werewolves were always on the verge of slipping into the monster, and that was what made them dangerous.

Another thing that the stories got wrong was the idea

that werewolves were mindless, murderous monsters when they were in their wolf form. If the change was provoked by anger or perception of danger, then they could certainly behave that way. If the werewolf chose to change, however, they remained largely in control. The thing that made transformed werewolves hazardous was that they had little to no concept of morality, no sense of what was right or wrong. There was only desire, and usually that desire was to kill.

That was where packs came in handy. Packs had a strict hierarchy mirroring that of regular wolves, with alphas in charge of the pack, betas below, and so on. Alpha werewolves had the ability to influence their pack members' decisions and could even force them out of transformation if necessary. Packs also offered support that werewolves didn't get on their own, such as experienced wolves that could teach control. And, more than that, they provided protection and a family.

For all of these reasons, werewolf packs were strictly illegal. There was no way for the government to be able to control alpha wolves and their packs, and they didn't want werewolves learning how to transform at will. They wanted werewolves to drink wolfsbane and stay as human as possible to make them less of a threat.

And if a werewolf didn't conform to this, they would be eliminated. Anita had grown up hearing horror stories from her grandfather of werewolves going out one night and never returning. She'd seen news stories of werewolves strung up in trees and hunted like animals. She'd received threats of the same from classmates and neighbors, and even teachers on occasion. So she had to try to be human, or she would be dead.

After a deep breath, Anita steeled her resolve and took a swig of the awful drink. It burned as it went down, and she refrained from gagging on it only due to years of taking it.

Already, she could feel her senses dimming and returning to a more human level. The miniscule cracks and grains in the bricks in front of her blurred away. The woman chatting on a cellphone to her divorce attorney four blocks left faded into the typical city atmosphere. The hot dog cart she smelled earlier blended back into the overbearing scent of car exhaust and city grime. The wolf inside drowsed and curled up to sleep.

Once Anita was sure she wasn't going to vomit, she slipped the flask back into her jacket and decided to head back out into the busy sidewalk. She knew the flier girl wouldn't follow her or point her out; there was a sort of unspoken code that humanoids didn't out other humanoids. Because of the stereotypes and negativity surrounding their kind, many tried to keep their true identities secret from people who didn't have to know. Werewolves and elves had it easiest, since they looked human most of the time, and the government hadn't yet started making them wear a symbol identifying them as humanoids. Others, like nymphs and centaurs, didn't have the ability to hide their identities since their physicality revealed them. They were always exposed.

Five minutes later, Anita was putting her key into her apartment door. The door across the hall opened a crack and old Mrs. Nedder glared her beady eyes at Anita, then scoffed and closed her door again. The *snitch* of locks latching was loud and purposeful, but Anita was used to Mrs. Nedder's daily ritual of disapproval and paid it no mind. Mrs. Nedder she could deal with. She was just glad she didn't run into Jeremy, the fifth grader that lived below her, who always tried to push her down the stairs while his mother laughed about how "boys will be boys."

Anita closed the door behind her and walked into her tiny studio apartment. She paused in concern as she dropped her keys on the grimy kitchen counter. Something was off. The air smelled of mold and plaster, which was the apartment, and of dark spices, which was her scent, but somehow the spice scent was different, as if there was something beneath it.

A cold breeze washed over her and brought with it the smell of the city outside. The sounds of traffic on the street below met her ears, and she realized that she must have left the window open when she left. That was probably the source of the strange smell; it was the city bleeding into her apartment. She walked to the other side of the apartment, through the small living room with the bathroom on the left and her bed around the corner. She closed the window and sighed, then turned to face her bed but saw that someone was already on it.

"Hello, Anita," the man said.

She inhaled, ready to scream, but he moved quickly off her bed and covered her mouth before she had the chance to.

"Don't. Scream," he said tersely, his lip curling.

The scream died in her throat but left her vocal cords tight with anxiety. She nodded dumbly, and the invader let her go and took a couple steps back from her. He was a white man, broad-shouldered and taller than her by several inches. His angular jaw was covered in stubble, and a long nose sat beneath deep set blue eyes that watched her sardonically. A smirk played at the edge of his lips, and a fang earring dangled from his left ear.

"You're quite difficult to track down, did you know that?" the man said casually, as if this were all normal and he hadn't broken into her apartment and told her not to scream.

"Who are you?" she asked through gritted teeth, clenching her fists at her sides and glancing around for anything she could possibly use as a weapon.

"Elijah Bennett," he replied, watching her glance around. "Looking for something to fight me off with?"

She ignored the question, though her face burned with embarrassment.

"You don't need to, you know. I'm not here to hurt you, Anita," he said.

"How do you know my name?" she asked, feeling

alarmed. After her grandfather had taken custody of her, they'd been put in a program similar to witness protection but was designed for survivors of creature attacks, and every time they moved they had to change identities. She'd been Maritza Atwell and Regina Caplin and Valeria May and many others, but she hadn't been Anita Doyle in a very long time.

"We're old friends," Bennett said sarcastically. "We go way back. About fourteen years, in fact."

Fourteen years. That was when—

"You—it's *you!*" she shrieked, backing up a few steps. The strange scent in the air finally made sense: he was a werewolf too. "You killed my family! You turned me!" she shouted, terror and rage forming a dangerous cocktail. She could feel the wolf start to claw her insides, but that wasn't right. She'd just taken the elixir; it shouldn't be stirring for at least half a day.

"Wrong and wrong," he replied with an impatient roll of his eyes. "I didn't kill your family, and I didn't turn you."

"But—" Her fingers fumbled at her chest, feeling for the thick white scars that laid there.

"I *am* the one that clawed you, but you can't be turned from a clawing," he said tiredly. "Come on, tell me: how does the werewolf virus get spread?"

"Blood and saliva," she answered robotically. It was a subject covered every year in school from kindergarten to senior year of high school: how to identify humanoids, and how to avoid becoming one if the state was transferable, like with werewolves and vampires.

"That's right. It's a blood disease, mutates your genetics, makes you a *monster*," Bennett said with a derisive sneer. "Now tell me, how does blood or saliva come from claws?"

The look he was giving her was one of extreme condescension, and one she had encountered far too much while growing up. It had always been a longshot that she was changed by claws. The police had speculated that drool had accidentally gotten in her wound, or perhaps the werewolf had purposefully mingled its blood with hers, but that was unlikely as it had nearly clawed her to death. In the end, they concluded it was a freak accident, emphasis on the *freak*.

"It doesn't," she snapped through gritted teeth. "But then, how am I—"

"You were born a werewolf, like me," he said grimly, "because you're my daughter."

Her mind hit a wall with that information. Even the wolf was stunned into immobility. She jumped instantly to the conclusion that he was lying; it was the only thing that made sense.

"You're crazy," she hissed.

"Perhaps," he allowed, "but it's true nonetheless."

Anita shook her head in denial. "Why were you there that night?" she asked angrily.

"To take you back," he said firmly, jaw clenched. "Your

bitch mother was a standard one-night-only while I was travelling cross-country. Six years later, I ran into her again by chance. Tried to hit her up for another round, but she refused 'cause apparently I got her knocked up the last time, and she had to give up the thing to a nice family across town. Poor girl had no idea what I was, or what you might be."

The gears in her mind turned agonizingly slowly. Her mouth was agape.

"You think you're surprised?" he said. "Imagine how I felt finding out I had pup."

"Then why come for me?" she exclaimed. "It had been six years. You could've let me be! Why did you track me down if you didn't want me?"

"Because we are pack," Bennett said, a righteous fire flaring in his pale blue eyes. "Wolves stick together, and I had to know if my mutation passed on to you. Us born wolves are different; the change comes at a different time for each of us. At the latest, the wolf awakens at puberty, but it can wake sooner in times of danger and high stress. Your so-called family wouldn't have been able to teach you control once you first transformed. They'd have shot you up full of the 'bane and kicked you to the curb."

"That's not true," she said, although that was almost exactly what her grandfather did.

"It *is* true," he insisted. "It happens all the time. It happened to me after my first change, and it would've happened to you. It happens to the bitten, too. Sooner or later, you gotta learn that the only people who care about werewolves are other werewolves. That's why we have to stick together. That's why I came for you, why I've been trying to find you since then." He stared at her and she tried not to shrink under his intense gaze. "I want you to come with me."

"So we can, what, form some sort of pack?" she asked, disgust squashing down the yearning that the wolf felt.

"I can help you," Bennett said, taking a step toward her. "I can teach you control. The wolfsbane is a band aid, a crutch. It's either going to stop working, or it's going to kill you."

The wolf paced circles inside her, and never before had she hated it so much.

His eyebrows raised. "It's already stopped working, hasn't it?"

"I don't know what you're talking about," she said quickly, her voice shooting up an octave.

"One of these days, they're going to do a test on you, and you're going to have too little of the drug in your system, and they're going to drag you away, and nobody will ever hear from you again," Bennett said, his voice dark and bitter. "There's a reason werewolves are only expected to live a max of twenty years after their first change. But if you come with me, you have a chance. You can be a real werewolf, Anita, not just a wolf in human's clothing."

"No. No way," she said, shaking her head. "You're

lying, about everything. You were there that night. You killed my family, and you tried to kill me."

"I didn't kill your family," he said impatiently, pinching the bridge of his nose.

"But you did try to kill me," she said almost triumphantly, glad that she had at least one detail right. That was, if he was telling the truth, which he probably wasn't.

"I was trying to stop you," he replied.

"Stop me," she repeated. "Stop me from what?"

"From killing me, too."

"Too?" Her brow furrowed, and then understanding oozed through her body like a sick poison, locking her limbs and stopping her heart.

"You think I killed my family," she whispered, appalled at the mere thought.

For the first time, something like pity entered Bennett's blue eyes.

"I *watched* you kill your family," he responded.

She took stumbling steps away from him, tripped on the edge of the rug, and fell to the floor. Bennett made no move to help her, only watched. She was glad he stayed away; she didn't know what she would do if he tried approaching her right now. The wolf was bristling, its hackles raised.

"Your emotions are pretty high right now. I could probably smell your anxiety from two blocks away," he said, slowly backing away from her. "So I'm gonna give you a chance to calm down and think rationally about joining me. I'm heading out of town tomorrow. Gonna stop by that rally before I go. If you're in, if you want to stop playing human, then come find me, and we'll go together. If you don't find me, well..." He sighed. "See you around, kid."

Bennett turned and headed toward the front door. She'd half-expected him to go through the window again. He paused and looked back at her. "You know, lone wolves are always the first ones to get picked off by the hunters."

"Then why are you alone?" she growled at him. "Where's *your* pack?"

He gave her a long, hard look, then opened the door and left.

The door clicked shut, and exhaustion hit her like a ton of bricks. She stayed down on the floor, overcome with thoughts and the struggle to keep the bile from rising in her throat. Standing would be too much of an effort right now.

Whenever Anita had heard others talk about traumatic events, they always said they could remember it so clearly, as if it had happened yesterday. Now more than ever, Anita wished that she could remember exactly what had happened. But it was like somebody had written her early memories down on a white board and then shoddily erased them, leaving bits and pieces.

The only solid details were that it was night, and her

family had been gathered in the living room, about to watch a movie. Her parents were snuggled on the couch, her older brother Teo sitting beside them, while Anita sat on the floor in a nest of blankets. Teo kept stealing handfuls of her popcorn despite having his own bowl. She couldn't remember the name of the movie or even what it was about, and for some reason that little detail drove her crazy, because there was nobody to ask. The only people who knew were six feet under in a plot two states over. They'd just started the movie, whatever it was, when the doorbell rang.

After that, Anita's memories were as jumbled and fragmented as a kaleidoscope. There was Papa's scream. A horrible gurgle. Mama's dead eyes. Red and blue lights flashing outside the window. Teo crumpled on the floor beside blood-speckled popcorn. The dark smell of musk. Spit dribbling down Anita's chin, her mouth stretched wide and screaming. A voice like bitter dark chocolate saying, "Hush, Anita," and then a terrible pain before it all went black.

A chill crept over her like a sweeping mist when she realized that the voice in her memories was the same as the voice that belonged to Bennett.

Anita got slowly to her feet and went over to her desk. She wrenched open the bottom drawer and pulled out a bunch of papers and newspaper clippings. Familiar headlines stared up at her: "Vicious Werewolf Attack Leaves Three Dead, Daughter Orphaned;" "Doyle

Daughter Turned by Family's Killer;" "Doyle Homicide Investigations Cease as Case Turns Cold." The trail for the murderer had gone dead quick, as there was no motive for any werewolves to target the Doyles, and there wasn't any evidence that pointed to a culprit. The only quirk about the case was that the claw marks on Anita's chest were deep, but the claw marks on the rest of the family were much shallower…

Nausea wrapped its fingers around Anita's throat, and she was forced to sit down again. The wolf was pacing circles inside of her, but she couldn't even imagine taking more wolfsbane right now with how queasy she already felt. A headache raged at her temples, shouting out all the questions she had, but there was nobody to answer them.

Her breath caught in her throat as she remembered the one person who might possibly know something: her grandfather.

Anita shifted her weight and pulled her cellphone out of her back jeans pocket. Her fingers trembled slightly over the touch screen, which mocked her indecision by reflecting her conflicted face in its blackness. She swallowed down her nerves and called her grandfather.

She waited with bated breath to see if he would pick up. The wolf perked its ears in anticipation. Each ring drove another nail into her skull, further enraging her already furious headache. She'd regretted calling him the moment she'd pressed the button, not wanting to face his quiet disappointment even just through a speaker, but her call would have already registered in his phone, so there was no going back.

By the fifth ring, she was beginning to hope she would only have to leave a voicemail, but, because this was her life and nothing ever went right, he picked up.

"*¿Qué quieres?*" her grandfather growled.

Ramiro Morales had wanted nothing to do with his only daughter Daria once she'd performed her final disobedience against him and ran off with Keelan Doyle, that *pinche cabrón*. The minute they'd eloped, he cut all contact, so one could imagine his surprise when the police contacted him ten years later and said he had to take custody of his granddaughter since a werewolf had killed her parents and brother and she had no other kin.

"*¿Qué?*" he barked again. "What?"

"I...I'm coming over," she said, suddenly having an urge to not have this conversation over the phone. "I need to talk to you."

There was a weighty pause, and then he grunted, followed by the click of hanging up.

Anita let out a breath and sagged for a moment before getting up from the floor. She grabbed her keys and walked down to the parking garage to drive out to her grandfather's house.

Life with her grandfather had been complicated to say the least. She'd never felt settled due to the constant moving around, and she had no support from him or anyone in her life. He'd always kept her at a distance despite her desire for any form of affection. He hated the fact that she was a werewolf, and, aside from when he was monitoring her wolfsbane intake, pretended that she was fully human. The way he had raised her was more like a warden than a grandfather, but she had to be grateful to him. If he hadn't taken her in, she could've gone into the foster system, and that was bad enough for human children. She often thought that the only reason he took her in was because she reminded him of her mother, but he rarely, if ever, talked about her. From what she could gather, their relationship had been tumultuous, since she had been a free spirit, and he was rather strict. Still, Anita had always been jealous of her classmates and their happy, loving, human families. There was nothing she wanted more than that.

The drive to her grandfather's house was only half an hour long, since he lived just on the outskirts of the city in order to keep an eye on her, but her anticipation made the minutes drag on. Despite the close proximity, they hardly had any contact. He called randomly every few months or so to check if she'd been taking the elixir, but that was about it. For her to call him, let alone to drive over, was unprecedented, and Anita was very nervous about it. She hadn't seen her grandfather in person in over a year.

By the time she finally pulled into the short driveway of her grandfather's house, it felt like almost an entire day had passed. She stepped out of the car into the evening air, took a swig of wolfsbane to be sure, and let herself in to the one-story house with the quaint garden in front.

"*¿Abuelo?*" she called shakily as she closed the door behind her, her voice slightly higher than usual.

"Living room," his gruff voice replied.

Her heart beat steadily increased in tempo with every step she took down the seemingly endless hall that led to the living room.

"Hello," she said shakily.

Her grandfather looked up at her from where he sat in his armchair. The skin on his grizzled face had started to sag more in the months that she hadn't seen him, but his dark eyes still held the same calculated disappointment that they always had. She swallowed resolutely and tried not to feel like she was eight years old again.

"Have you been taking your elixir?" he asked predictably.

Anita repressed a sigh. "Yes."

"*Bueno*. What did you need to talk about?"

"Am I adopted?" she blurted.

What she'd meant to ask first was how much he knew about the night of the attack, how much he knew about the mysterious werewolf that had killed her family, but this turned out to be the question at the front of her mind.

The corners of his thin mouth turned down in suspicion. "*Sí*."

The urge to vomit returned as her thoughts spun dizzily in her head. Bennett had at least been telling the truth about that. If she truly was adopted, then maybe she really was his daughter, and maybe he was telling the truth about what—

"I found out when I received your records after taking custody. I chose not to tell you so to not take away the family you already lost," her grandfather elaborated, and she faintly realized that was probably the kindest thing he'd ever done for her. "How did you find out?"

Bennett's face flashed in her mind's eye.

"Did you ever try to track down my birth parents?" she asked instead of answering.

He sighed. "*Sí.*"

Her heart pounded heavily. "And?"

"I found your birth mother," he replied. "She lived across town, worked as a waitress. The father was never around. She only knew his first name, Eli. You were an accident."

Worry tangled itself in her stomach. Eli could have been short for Elijah, an alias to keep his identity private.

"*¿Abuelo,*" she said, "how was I turned?"

His eyes darkened the way they always did when she brought up her lycanthropy. The topic had always been forbidden in their household, aside from when he was asking about the wolfsbane or lecturing her about werewolves gone astray.

"The werewolf who killed your family clawed and turned you," he said, just as he had all her life.

"Except you don't believe that," she said slowly, amazed at her daring, "do you?"

His eyes narrowed. "What are you hinting at?"

"Is it possible that I was born a werewolf?" she asked.

"I suppose," he answered.

"Am I…am I the one?" she asked, her throat seizing up. "The one who—"

Her grandfather's eyes watched her for a very long time. Anita could remember looking into those eyes and waiting to see a smile in them, waiting for some form of caring.

"*Creo que sí,*" he said finally. *I believe so.*

Her heart dropped into her stomach, and the wolf sat up. Tears burned in her eyes and she raised shaking hands to her head, pressing at her temples in an effort to try to regain some focus.

"You knew—you *knew*—" she stammered, swaying heavily on her feet.

"I had my suspicions," he corrected, watching her carefully, "but there was no way to be sure. So I made it my mission to eradicate the wolf inside you. I tried to make you human, so you would never kill again—"

"But I'm *not* human!" she screamed. "You can't kill the wolf! Wolfsbane isn't a cure, it's a band aid!" Dimly, she realized she was echoing Bennett's words.

"Where is this coming from?" he demanded angrily as he rose to his feet. "What's gotten into you?"

"You were so unfair to me," she hissed, "expecting me to be something I couldn't. Why couldn't you accept me as I was?"

"Accept you? You, *muchacha del diablo*?" he snarled, disgust curling his lip as he used his favorite nickname for her. "You are *¡una monstruo*! *¡Una bruja!* You killed your own family, my only daughter! I tried to save you, tried to—"

"There's no saving me!" she exclaimed, her voice shrill. "There's no changing what I am, *¡Abuelo!*"

The wolf was growling, pawing the edges, waiting to be released. Anita could feel bloodlust humming in her fingertips, fueled by all this resentment she'd held in for years. She felt the desire to crush her grandfather's skull and see his blood soak the carpet.

She wrenched herself out of that mindset, shocked at herself.

"I-I need to go," she said quickly, then turned and ran.

"Anita, get back here!" he shouted, moving after her. "Anita!"

Anita threw the front door open and jumped into her car, fingers fumbling with getting the key in the ignition. The wolf snarled and barked, mad and foaming with violent rage, and she could feel it scratching at the surface.

"Anita, stop! *¡Para!*" her grandfather yelled, approaching her car.

She finally started the car and peeled out of the driveway, speeding down the street and around the corner back toward the heart of the city. The wolf howled furiously now, and she could feel the control slipping from her. Her vision was going fuzzy at the edges, and her skin kept itching like it was about to sprout fur. Hurriedly, she wrenched the steering wheel and pulled over to the side of the road. With shaking fingers, she grabbed her flask and guzzled the rest of the elixir that was in it.

Anita pressed her forehead against the steering wheel and squeezed her eyes shut, then focused on breathing slowly and calming her emotions down as the wolfsbane coursed through her system. The anger disappeared more quickly than she thought it would, and it left her exhausted and weak. The wolf curled up reluctantly, but its ears were still perked.

Bennett was right: the wolfsbane wasn't working anymore, and Anita was terrified to imagine what would happen the next time she got angry. She had just been on the verge of killing her own grandfather. If she could do that, what else was she capable of? Who else would she hurt? Who else would she *kill?*

Hot tears slid down her cheeks. She had to learn control, but how? From Bennett? And what if she was never able to learn control? What if the wolf—the monster—was untamable?

Anita sat in her car and cried until the last rays of sunlight left the sky. Numbly, she started the car again and drove the rest of the way back, but when she arrived in the parking garage, she couldn't even remember the drive. Her mind was so frazzled from everything that had happened that day that it couldn't focus on anything. A tightness had spread through her body, making it hard to move and breathe, let alone think. How had it only been mere hours since Bennett showed up in her apartment?

When she finally managed to drag her weary feet up the stairs to her apartment, she spied something stuck to her door.

It was a rally flier, declaring that "WE ARE ALL EQUAL."

She ripped it off and crumpled it into a ball, then slammed her door behind her.

Anita spent the rest of the night and most of the next day curled up in a lump on her bed. She'd considered lighting a candle and praying for guidance, but she hadn't been in contact with God since her grandfather had taken her to a priest who'd claimed he could 'convert' her from werewolf to human. It had been traumatic to say the least, and she hadn't stepped foot near a church in over ten years.

Instead, she lay in her bed and drifted in and out of consciousness, lost in a haze of confusion. Dreams were interspersed throughout the blackness, scattered memories of the night of her family's murder coming back to her. There was a pair of hands on each of her arms, pulling her in two different directions. Bennett standing in the living room, purple with rage and yelling in Papa's face. Mama on the floor, staring up in horror, with Teo's body lying next to her. A reflection in the polished wood of their piano of a small werewolf with bloodied claws—

Anita woke in a cold sweat, sitting up instantly. There were dried tear tracks on her puffy face, and she felt utterly ragged, like fabric that had been stretched too thin. A glance at the clock on her bedside table told her it was almost eight at night. The rally would be starting soon.

She pressed the heels of her hands into her eyes and tried not to panic at the choice that was now looming directly before her. Would she go to the rally and leave with Bennett? Or would she stay and let him leave without her?

She took a breath. She let it out. She got out of bed.

Ten minutes later, Anita's breath formed clouds in front of her face and she found herself approaching the city square that sat directly in front of the city hall building. It was a large square, the size of two city blocks, with a playground and a grassy area specifically for dogs. The center of it was wide and paved and lined with trees. A stage was set up at the far end with City Hall behind it, the domed stone building making an impressive backdrop. Two tall banners with Senator Irving's face and the saying "EQUALITY NOW" were on either side of the stage, and a podium sat in the middle. Floodlights cast a harsh light into the autumn darkness.

The crowd was impressively large, and the atmosphere felt tense and full of fervent activism. Anita briefly wondered what would happen if that tension spilled over. She'd never seen so many humanoids gathered in one place before. The scent of werewolves was heavy on the air, making it impossible for Anita to pick out Bennett. A small coven of vampires stood together holding a sign that said "We don't suck—YOU do." She spied a group of wood nymphs that had gathered together, their skin like tree bark. There were several centaurs that stood on the edge of the crowd, pawing nervously at the ground. Anita hadn't seen a centaur since she'd gone to the fair when she was nine and there was one forced into giving "pony rides." Sprites glittered in the air like multicolored fireflies. Every now and then they spelled out words like "equality" or "rights for all." All these and more were gathered tonight.

The bell tower in City Hall chimed eight, and Senator Irving stepped onto the stage.

As Irving walked up to the podium, everybody started screaming and clapping and stomping their excitement. Several different chants started up, the conflicting beats and words creating nothing but chaotic shouting.

"Quite the commotion here, isn't it?"

Anita whirled around in terror and found Bennett standing behind her, his mouth twisted in a wolfish grin. Irving raised her hand to silence the crowd, and then her voice floated over the crowd.

"Never before has our kind been so united!" Irving declared. "I don't see vampires, selkies, and fairies out here tonight. I see my siblings who have struggled alongside me under the humans' oppression!"

The crowd gave a mighty cheer, and Bennett rolled his

eyes. Anita was too panicked and conflicted to pay attention to the speech.

"So, do you wanna stick around for the rest of this or skip out now?" Bennett asked. "Probably best if we go now. Beat the traffic and all."

"I-I'm not going with you," she said, clenching her fists.

Bennett raised his eyebrows.

"I was five years old when my seal skin was stolen from me," Irving continued over them, "preventing me from ever returning to the ocean I called home…"

"Then why come?" he asked. "Unless you really wanted to hear the speech."

"I wanted to see you one last time," she replied. She licked her lips and swallowed. "For, uh, closure and all that. To…to look you in the face and tell you no."

"Too long have we been hated for what we cannot control, generalized and grouped under the label "dangerous"!" Irving shouted, and resounding cheers came up from the crowd.

Bennett nodded slowly. "Right. You want to know what I think?"

She shook her head fearfully.

"I think you do want to come with me," he said. "You're just too scared."

Alarm gripped her as denial flooded her senses. "No, no, that's not—"

"This is for the sirens, with their vocal cords removed!

For the werewolves, forced to drink their poison! For the fairies, shackled in iron! For the centaurs, treated as cattle! This is for all of us! We will be silent no more! You will hear us! You will know us!"

"Anita, you have to understand," Bennett said. "Control isn't an option, it's a necessity."

"I've been managing fine," she replied shakily, but the wolf inside her was grinning.

"We demand equality!" Irving bellowed.

The crowd started chanting. "Equality! Equality! Equality!"

Bennett opened his mouth to speak but was drowned out by police sirens.

"This is the city police!" said a voice on a megaphone. "Disband and go home immediately or face legal consequences."

A wall of police officers with riot shields started to surround the crowd. They beat their batons against the shields, making the humanoids near them rustle nervously.

"We are here peacefully protesting," Irving said tersely into the microphone.

Anita couldn't tell if she was upset that the police were here or upset that they had interrupted her speech.

"This protest has become violent. You are ordered to leave now," the voice replied.

"Vio—" Irving started, but was cut off by a scream.

Anita couldn't tell what happened, but suddenly the

line of police started charging the crowd. The centaurs scattered in terror, and people scrambled to get out of their way and to escape the approaching police force. The pushing and shoving caused people to fall to the ground and get trampled. Anita's heart jumped in her throat as she was shoved to the side into more passing bodies, and the wolf tensed its muscles. She had no choice but to move with the crowd.

People started screaming in terrible pain, and Anita strained her neck to see the cause. The police were armed with what looked like iron and silver batons. She saw one threatening a vampire with a wooden stake. Handcuffs glinted all over the place as people were dragged off. One centaur was on its back and hogtied. Something exploded in the air, and from the taste and lack of smell, Anita could tell it was an aconite gas bomb.

"Anita!" Bennett called, pushing his way toward her. "Let's—"

The people near her scattered, and she ran into a hard body. She looked up and met the hateful eyes of one of the police officers. He grabbed her roughly.

"You're under arrest for unlawful assembly and interference with police authority," he announced.

"Get off of me!" Anita shouted, pulling herself out of his grip.

The officer raised his baton—she recognized it as silver—and struck her across the face with it. The silver burned her skin in addition to the crushing pain of the blow, and without warning, the wolf exploded out of her. Fur burst up along her arms and her clothes ripped as her body morphed. Pain lit her up from the inside out as her bones snapped and grew.

Werewolves were much larger than regular wolves, standing close to seven feet tall when on their hind legs. Everything about them was longer and sharper and deadlier. Their fangs and claws were inches long and sharper than knives. Strength poured from every tensed muscle. Senses were tripled with sharp eyes, sharp ears, and an even sharper nose.

Anita's mind went blank as the wolf took over, seething with fury. She faced the man, who was cowering before her, holding the silver baton above his head in fear.

She took a breath and roared in his face, spittle flying from her gums. Her vision was tinged red, and she raised her paw to strike him like he'd struck her—

Suddenly, the present left her. She was six years old and her parents were about to watch a movie. *The Wizard of Oz,* the television screen read. Bennett was there, barging into the living room. He grabbed Anita by the arm and tried dragging her out of the house, but her dad grabbed her too. Something in her was scratching its way out, and she had no way to stop it. It got the better of her and jumped out, then—

Anita gasped and wrenched her body back away from the police officer. The wolf whined in disgruntled surprise and immediately tried to resume control. She stumbled away, breathing heavily, trying to fight the desire to tear something's throat out.

"*No!*" Bennett shouted suddenly.

A shot went off, and two bodies hit the ground as screams went up all around them. Anita turned, her werewolf eyes allowing her to easily see what was happening in the night air. Bennett was on top of the officer, wrestling the man's gun out of his hands. He punched the man hard, and the officer went still. Bennett thrust the gun into his jeans and got up, approaching Anita slowly.

She growled instinctively, but he reached up and grabbed her muzzle, baring his human teeth at her. The wolf struggled for a moment, then met Bennett's eyes and started to calm down. The transformation released her, and she was human again in moments.

"Come on," Bennett said. He grabbed her arm and began shoving his way through the still panicking though severely diminished crowd. Anita was too dizzy and drained from her recent transformation to do anything but clutch her torn clothes and run.

A few blocks later they spun around a corner and into the doorway of an abandoned hotel. Together they crouched in their hiding place, trying to catch their breath.

"You were going to kill that man," Bennett said after a moment.

Anita flinched, and shame burned a hole in her chest. She put her head down and wrapped her arms around her knees. She felt a jacket settle around her shoulders and a hand press lightly on her arm.

"You were going to kill him, but you didn't," he amended. "You stopped yourself."

"Barely," she gasped, heaving sobs shaking her body. "I…I remembered that n-night, I remembered…I-I remember the g-goddamn movie…," she cried. "I remember w-wanting to kill my f-family, just like I wanted to k-kill that officer."

"You didn't want to kill that man," he said, "the wolf did."

"What's the difference?" she snapped, raising her head to glare tearfully at him.

"It's all the difference in the world," he replied firmly. "That's what the humans don't understand about us. Control isn't about choosing the human over the wolf. It's about accepting both, about finding the balance between them."

"But it's a monster," she countered, shaking her head. "I'm a monster."

"We're all capable of being monsters," he declared, eyes flashing. "Even the humans. *Especially* the humans. The wolf isn't a monster, Anita. It's just a wolf."

She looked up at him.

He watched her steadily. "And I can help you to control it. You don't need to be scared of it anymore."

Anita closed her eyes and pursed her lips. She thought of all the years she'd lived in fear. Fear of being killed, fear of killing, fear of the monster that lived inside her. Fear was no way to live, and she was more terrified now than she ever had been. And it seemed the only solution was the brusque man that was sitting before her. She could either stay in the city downing wolfsbane till she died or the government took her, or she could leave with Bennett and have a chance at finally controlling the wolf. And if there was any chance at all, even a slim one, didn't she have to take it?

A memory came back to her, a long-forgotten dream of what it would be like to run wild and free. She wondered what it would be like to live without fear of others, without fear of herself. She dreamed of meeting other werewolves and forming a pack. She would be loved and accepted for who she was—wolf and all—but that dream had long since been discarded.

Except…

Bennett sighed in frustrated aggravation at her silence. "Dammit! I'm not good at this stuff, but I'm your fucking father, Anita, and I'm not going to let you keep living like this! I know you're scared right now, but learning control is worth it. It's the only way. Listen, we can stay in the city if you want, but it'll be easier if we're isolated. Less people to possibly hurt. We could live in the woods, or I can track down the pack that taught me, or—"

"Okay."

He paused. "What?"

"Okay," she repeated, looking up. She took a deep

breath. "I'll go with you."

Bennett sagged with relief and his grin was back. "Good. We should—"

"I'll go with you, but you're not my father," she said firmly. "My father was Keelan Doyle, not you."

"That's fine," he replied, nodding. "But we are blood."

She raised her chin, and he leaned forward, moonlight hitting the side of his pale face.

"We are pack."

There was something about the way he said it that made her shiver. It sounded like something sacred.

Pack. The word entered her chest and settled heavily in her stomach, sending warmth throughout her body. It gave her a sense of grounding she'd never felt before. The wolf rose to its feet, and for the first time, she didn't feel as if it was working against her. Anita sat up a little taller and looked Bennett straight in the eye.

She nodded. "We are pack."

The wolf tipped its head back and howled.

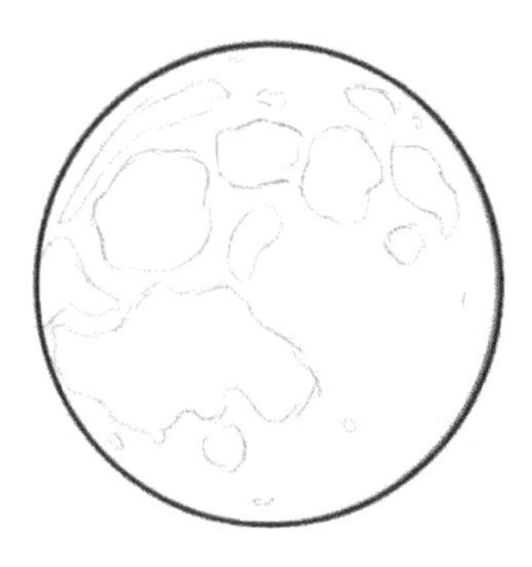

Mother Nature...Mother Nurture

Lizzy Carney

I am losing my mother in pieces. She is like an autumn tree: beautiful, colorful, yet dying. The breeze of Alzheimer's whispers through the branches while her memory drops off with the leaves.

One day, when her tree is finally bare, I will hold a memory of her blooming strength. She weathered the storms and provided me with shelter. I will be strong and remain hopeful because of her. For now, I will hope for spring to come, so together we may see the blossoms and green growth of love.

On a September drive through the Oregon wine country, Mom asked me, "What will we see once the leaves have all fallen?" She answered her own question. "Skeleton trees?"

I gather what is falling: her stories, her looks, her insights, and her love. Nature's beauty is my rake. I rake these moments we share, embracing them as simple gifts of beauty.

Another day she smiles and says, "Oh, the little fast birds are here." I look up to the fuchsia hanging in the window and see the swift messengers of love and joy. Hummingbirds never seem to stop, never glide. I will them to linger. I will life to linger, to be savored, so that we can take our time and drink the nectar. I know that hummingbirds symbolize immortality, bravery, joy, and perseverance. I wonder if their flight of infinity would journey into our house and allow me to have my mom a little longer. These tiny creatures delight her with their fleeting visits and provide me with a sense of peace, knowing that I will never stop savoring the nectar of my mom's sweetness.

We rest on her bed with eyes wide and focused out the window and on the sky. The clouds drift. Mom comments that the sun is warm and melting the clouds. She asks what I see…I say I see a cloud passing as a caterpillar.

"No," she says, "it is God reaching out to us."

We are quiet as the view changes. She pities the person without imagination. The sky's stage provides for an ensemble of characters: herds of wild animals stampede across the horizon. Musical instruments silently blow to the west. Stout kings float by followed by soaring chubby cherubs.

"The clouds are heavy," she remarks. "It will rain, and they will be lighter."

I feel her love and bask in the slow motion of the

moment. The clouds are dark and threatening. Mom dozes; I keep my eye on the clouds, waiting for one to pass and offer me a silver lining. I will be patient.

"How many sunsets have we watched together?" Mom asks me. Before I can respond, she muses, "The sky is a Van Gogh painting, only more beautiful." She holds my hand while we wait and watch colors transform the sky into impressionistic images. Sunset...a day's end, bringing breathtaking moments of change in us, entwined with nature.

The sun is setting on my mother. The hues and tones of her life dim quietly as the dusk of the disease sets in on her memories. I cling to the colors of our time now. I embrace the brushstrokes of the afterglow and realize that twilight is approaching and then will come darkness.

Magically, clouds part for the moon. The fuzziness of the veiled moon has cleared, and so a bright glow streams down upon us as our night light. We watch the moon rise while the stars decorate the sky. We talk as if we are young girls on a sleepover.

Mom wonders if Ireland has a moon. She did not see it when we were there last. I assure her Ireland has a moon, and it is the same one we are viewing this night. We tease about shooting for the moon, and that if we miss, we will hit a star. Together we count and wish and wonder.

One day I will look at the world for both of us: capturing the beauty in my heart; wishing on the giggling stars; watching the sun playing "sneak and peek." My heart is broken as I lose my mother in pieces, watching the woman who was my mother disappearing leaf by leaf. It is broken open with love. I smile, stirring up memories of the joys we share overseeing the birds, sunsets and the night skies together, embracing Mother Nature. Smiling for the many joys we have had together.

Grief changes us forever. There is never 'normal' again. But my sorrowful and changed spirit will remember that I carry within me the beauty of my mother. She will be with me always, and I will be healed by the memories of ordinary and extraordinary moments we shared with nature. Mom will always nurture me. The moon will trade places with the sun, and in my darkness I know morning will come.

I recall Carl Sandburg's line, "The moon is a friend for the lonesome to talk to." My mother's moon and I will be having many conversations.

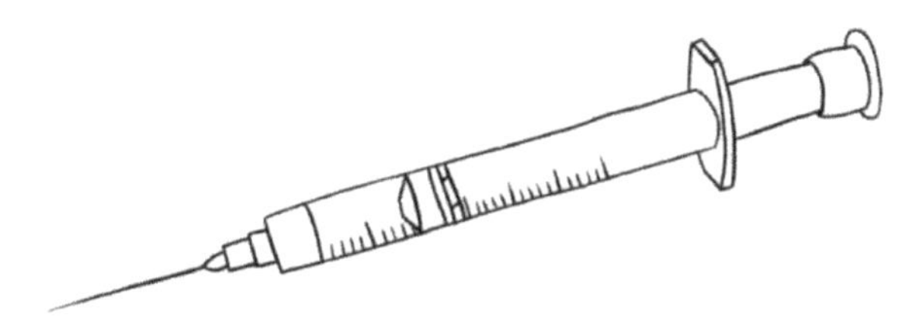

Zombie Apocalypse Rescue Agency

LeeAnn McLennan

"Oh man." Lark punched the red button to silence the alarm echoing through the office. She hated the bleeping noise almost more than the ever-lurking zombies. "We got another shiver requesting a pickup."

Lark managed to hide most of her sneer, but her co-worker, Tony, frowned at her while reaching for olive green Kevlar coverall sporting the logo identifying them as employees of the Zombie Apocalypse Rescue Agency, ZARA for short.

"Don't call them shivers." Tony zipped up his coverall and began pulling out his weapons from his locker.

Lark shrugged into her own coverall, made of a slick bite-repelling fabric. "Why not? It's what they want, to get picked up so they can sit in a bunker and shiver in fear." She checked her own weapons. "They've had enough of waiting for the zombie freaks to die off or disappear or whatever sad belief they follow. So they call us. We pick them up, take them to a safe bunker, they hide out, all safe and sound, but shivering."

"They pay the company a large sum of money for our

services." If it was possible to look prim while checking an automatic, Tony did.

Lark strapped on her gun belt and added a gun to each holster. She missed Jake, her old partner, but Jake got himself munched a few runs ago when they'd gone out to pick up a local TV star. Jake had gotten flirty with the barely legal girl and didn't see the cluster of zombies, maybe an old fan club, converging on them. Lark managed to get the shivering starlet into the armored truck but the last she'd seen of Jake was his legs twitching as the brain eaters chomped on him.

Lark hoped Jake was dead. She didn't relish giving her old friend a head shot should they meet again. She'd do it, of course, but she would feel bad.

"Ready?" Tony was done with his weapons check, loaded for bear, and waited by the door. Lark tucked a knife in her boot and followed Tony out of the control room. Jack and Ryan, their replacements, passed them going in.

Big Bessie sat in the garage with all the other armored trucks. Modified from the design used for armored vans, ZARA's trucks had solid, steel plated exteriors, with guns mounted on top, front, sides, and back. The driver sat in the front cab, the gunner sat in the back—a steel wall with a door set between the driver's and passenger's seats separated the front from the back. During pickup runs, the gunner locked themself in the back. Once they got to the shiver, the driver retrieved and handed the shiver off to the gunner. The shiver and the gunner stayed locked in the back until they got back to HQ. If the driver was compromised, the gunner and the shiver could hold out in the back of the truck until help came. Lark had only needed to do that once; she still had nightmares about spending three hours with a hysterical middle-aged trust fund guy. The shiver had yelled and threatened to sue the company for failing to provide better service. After an hour, Lark was ready to shove the guy outside to take his chances. Only the camera recording the van stopped her. The punishment for deliberately endangering a client was to get put on foot patrol around the boundaries of North Portland, now called Z-town, where the zombies were the heaviest.

When she was the shooter on a pickup run, Lark controlled the many guns bristling around the exterior using a system modified from old game controllers. She could pop off zombies from all sides without ever leaving the safety of Big Bessie. Just like playing first person shooter games as a teenager.

Usually the sight of Big Bessie made Lark feel safe and smug, but lately…no. She wasn't turning into a shiver, not her. She reached inside her unzipped coverall and pulled out a quarter, a currency useless now except for wishing wells or coin tosses. "Heads, I'm shooter."

Tony gave an irritated jerk of his head. He didn't approve of Lark's method of determining who drove and who shot. Tony preferred they alternate between roles, but that was boring to Lark.

"Ha!" Lark grinned when the quarter landed heads up. Tony just sighed and got into the driver's side.

Lark climbed into the back via the door in the cab. She settled into the gunner's seat, zipped up her coverall, and pulled up the gun controller system to run the standard pre-run systems diagnostics.

While the diagnostics ran, Lark leaned through the still open door. "Hey Tony, who's our shiver?"

Tony switched on Big Bessie's ignition to warm up the truck. "Our *customer* is named Bailey Johnson." Tony peered at his monitor as the coordinates for their destination came up. "Uh, okay, that's unusual. He lives in Buckman."

In the act of buckling in, Lark stopped and stared at the monitor, certain Tony had made a mistake, an unprecedented event to be sure, but there was always a first time. But the blinking red dot signaling their pickup was firmly in the Buckman neighborhood.

"That doesn't make any sense." Lark closed her eyes tight then opened them wide. "No one in that neighborhood has the money to buy ZARA"

The company's services were crazy expensive; only the filthy rich could manage the cost, though some people managed to negotiate the service into their job contracts in lieu of bonuses. Most pickups were in the fortified neighborhoods in the 'burbs or in some of the fancy protected condos along the waterfront.

Ten years ago, the zombies started showing up, seemingly out of nowhere. One day there were a few zombies shuffling around; most people thought it was a typical Portland event—a zombie walk or something. That is, until the creatures started munching on people. Then it got real, real fast.

Even then, it took a few years before the creatures became a true national menace. Some scientists studied them and declared that even though zombies were dangerous because they wanted to chomp your brains—earning them the nickname brain munchers—it was actually quite rare for the virus that made them to be transferred. People infected with it usually died.

The term 'zombies' wasn't even the correct name since the creatures weren't really back from the dead; the virus simply gave them the characteristics usually associated with zombies. People still called them zombies, though. The zombies were treated sort of like violent meth heads—best to be avoided but not about to take over. Some labs on the East Coast devoted their time to studying them, looking for a cure.

At least, that's how it started. In the past few years, the virus had gotten stronger. Now, if you got bit it was a 9 out of 10 chance you'd Z-out. So people started taking precautions. If you were lucky enough to sell armored trucks, guns, ammo, you got rich overnight. Knowing how to zombie-proof a house became a top profession. Most companies enforced a work-from home policy.

Delivery services blossomed overnight, and delivery people were acclaimed for their bravery—or stupidity, depending who you asked. People became less and less willing to go out to concerts, movie theatres, anywhere there might be crowds hiding zombies. Most events were held via Internet streaming now.

Lark hadn't been across the Willamette River to the eastside of Portland in about eight years. She still missed the cozy craftsman home she'd grown up in, but it wasn't fortified. And, anyway, her mother had been killed in the kitchen by a neighbor who'd Z-ed out in front them, so Lark didn't want to go back.

For some reason, in Portland, the brain munchers proliferated the eastside across the river from downtown. No one knew why, or if they did, they hadn't told Lark. All she knew was no one went across the river unless they had a good reason. And most people didn't have a good reason. Only two of the seven bridges spanning the Willamette remained—the Marquam and the Burnside Bridges. Luckily the Burnside would take them near enough to the Buckman neighborhood, but it was still riskier than a west side pickup. Lark had heard the industrial area just across the bridge was majorly infested. Thank goodness zombies couldn't swim.

None of those facts changed how unusual it was to get a pickup on the eastside of Portland. Lark hadn't heard of one in years, and that pickup had been a disaster—ending with the pickup guys and the shiver all getting Z-ed out.

"Well damn." Lark reached for the helmet she didn't always bother wearing when she was the gunner on a run. "I guess we'd better get this over with."

Tony had already fastened his helmet with its fitted collar around his neck. He hadn't lowered the face plate, and Lark could see the sweat on his upper lip. "Ready?"

Lark nodded and reached for the heavy door between the front cab and the back of the truck. She hesitated before saying the benediction she used to give Jake when he drove while Lark literally rode shotgun. "Safe driving, clear roads."

Tony put his hand on his face shield, his eyes meeting Lark's in the mirror. "Good shooting." Tony flipped the shield down as Lark secured the door, locking herself in the back. She shifted in her seat as Big Bessie started moving out of the underground garage and up the five levels to the heavily guarded entrance of the downtown high-rise/underground bunker that was ZARA's headquarters. All employees lived and worked in the well-protected building, which included a dining and shopping district spanning several floors.

Lark heard Tony radioing the guards and telling them to expect an authorized exit. Lark switched on the three monitors: one showing the back of Tony's head in the cab, one showing alternating exterior views, and the last one showing nothing of interest…yet. All too soon that monitor would show the weird zombie heat signature indicating where to shoot.

Lark felt Big Bessie rumble over the metal grating near the exit gate. She watched the monitors as the guard waved them out into the deserted streets. Rain gleamed off the pavement. It was nighttime; only a few diehards would be outside trying to prove how badass they were—no cowering inside away from the dark streets for them. That is, until one of their buddies got munched. That usually converted them to escapism inside. Occasionally, the experience had the opposite effect—turning the witness into a vigilante who spent nights offing zombies; usually getting offed themselves sooner or later.

In Lark's opinion, most people should just make the best of life while waiting for the frequently-promised cure. Not that she really believed in a cure. No, Lark believed in Big Bessie and her guns, that was pretty much it.

Lark felt the truck lurch. She automatically checked the heat sig monitor before Tony radioed back. "Bunch of zombies. Gear up."

Lark wrapped her hands around the gun controller, "Yeah, okay. On it."

Lark felt so freaking powerful as she blasted the brain munchers into bloody bits, though a tiny part whispered that it would be more visceral to make the kill shots in the open air. She steadfastly ignored the voice; she was safer inside Big Bessie. And the goal was the pickup, not killing zombies. That was someone else's job.

"Heading over the Burnside Bridge," Tony announced.

Lark shifted in her seat, her shoulders tightening, anticipating many more zombies ahead.

Tony exchanged words with the ever-present bridge guards. One of them said, "Man, that sucks. We're hearing reports it's getting worse over there. You know we'll have to test you when you come back."

Lark mentally seconded Tony's surprised, "What?" The test was a quick skin prick, like the TB test. It only took twenty seconds to confirm non-zombie status, but it was a long-ass twenty seconds. Lark didn't know things had gotten so bad that the bridge guards were administering the test. As employees of ZARA, they were always tested after a shiver run, so she was used to it, the cold prick, the waiting, the relief...so far. Still, it was unsettling knowing the bridge guards found it necessary for all eastside excursions now.

As Big Bessie rolled across the Burnside Bridge, Lark found herself wishing she was driving so she could see the terrain with her own eyes, not through the monitors. She remembered how pretty the city had looked at night before. Light from buildings and bridges reflecting off the water; people walking and biking through the streets; cars with windows open taking people to dinner or the movies, somewhere fun and carefree. On second thought, she was glad the monitors didn't show great detail. She liked her memories better.

"We're over." Tony's announcement made Lark's stomach twist. "Over the bridge, turning right on MLK.

Not much activity but stay alert."

Lark snorted. Like she was napping back here. She scanned the area with the heat sig monitor while keeping an eye on the exterior cameras. Tony was right; not many zombies showed on the heat sig scan. And those that did shambled along in the direction Tony drove. Lark blasted them, proving to Tony she was vigilant.

Big Bessie maneuvered past abandoned cars, around huge potholes, over a fallen telephone pole. The old Subaru dealership where she'd bought her first new car was torn all to hell—cars with busted windows rusting in the rain.

Lark leaned back, stretching her already stiff arms, when Big Bessie slammed to a stop. Lark was thrown forward, the straps of her seat belt biting into her chest, whacking her head on the wall in front of her.

"Tony, what the hell?"

"Shut up and look." Tony's voice shook, freaking Lark out more than the sudden stop.

Lark jerked the heat sig monitor closer and stared at it. "Holy hell, there must be hundreds of them." Ahead of them, on MLK, the heat sig was a solid mass of teeming red. It looked like they were all moving in fits and starts down MLK in the direction of Stark. Pretty much right in the path Big Bessie needed to go. The pickup destination was up Stark about fifteen blocks, near the Lone Fir Cemetery around 20th.

Lark's mind shrank away from the idea of busting

through the seething mob, even in Big Bessie with her guns blasting away front, back, and sideways. To get through all of that mess, they needed a convoy of Big Bessies.

If it was like this all the way to the shiver's place, then Lark actually felt some sympathy for the poor soul.

"What do you think?" Lark asked Tony. They didn't have the option of turning back; it was against company policy. They had to get to the shiver—it was a matter of doing it alone or waiting for reinforcements. No one had ever called for backup; Lark really didn't want to be the first but then, to her knowledge, no one had ever faced this many zombies at once. Still, it sucked; she'd never hear the end of it back at the tower.

"I'll call HQ. At least they can find out how deep the infestation is." Headquarters had wider range scanners than the trucks. "See if there's a better route."

"Good plan. Get on it." Lark focused on the heat sig monitor, expecting any moment for the hoard to turn on Big Bessie, but the mass kept moving towards Stark. It looked like more zombies were joining the slow march. Lark had never seen brain eaters organize like this. She really hoped the creatures weren't getting smart.

Tony spoke up, sounding a little bit calmer. "Okay, they're running a wide scan." ZARA had set up sensors all around Portland, partnering with some of the security companies. "Looks like the zombies are mostly heading up Stark. Not sure why. It looks like we can detour around the main group if we head up MLK to Hawthorne." He paused as if listening. "And come in down 20th. HQ says we'll have to go through some clumps but not like this. They don't think we need any reinforcements. Ready?"

Tony didn't wait for Lark's reply before backing up and roaring down MLK. Lark tightened her seatbelt with one hand while watching the monitors. The truck leapt into the air, dropping back the ground hard enough to jar Lark to her teeth.

"Hang on, just had to drive over a few." Tony said. "Get ready, more coming up."

Lark rolled her eyes. She knew there were zombies coming their way; they popped up on the monitor. She aimed the guns and blew them to pieces. The rapid *rat-tat* of her guns relaxed her. She was back in control.

Big Bessie barreled up the ramp from MLK to Hawthorne, Lark popping off zombies as quickly as possible. In her hearts of hearts, she was glad she couldn't make out their faces. One of her recurring nightmares was of offing a friend or family member. After all, she had no clue what happened to her junkie father. She figured if she had to shoot her dad or worse, her old partner Jake, she'd rather not know. One less zombie was the point; it wasn't like she could help her Dad if the old guy had been Z-ed.

Lark swayed with Big Bessie as Tony swerved onto 20th. For the moment it was quiet. Lark tensed. This was usually when things tipped over into crazy. Quiet before the storm kinda thing. The chest strap of her seatbelt cut into her chest, and she realized she was straining forward as if she could see through the steel door. She gave a half-laugh and leaned back. She wasn't the one in this truck who should fret. Tony was more vulnerable; no matter how glass was treated, it was never going to be stronger than steel.

She settled back, checking the monitors—still clear, completely clear, crazy unusual. Normally a run was a steady series of popping off zombies in ones and twos. This run was feast or famine. Lark chuckled at her gruesome joke.

"Tony, how ya doing up there?" Lark didn't want Tony to get too relaxed. Though Tony was wound pretty tight, so it might be an improvement.

"Yeah, I'm good. Weird run, huh?"

"Too right. Stay sharp."

Tony just grunted in response. Big Bessie rumbled up 20th, slowing as they neared Belmont. "Lark, do you see this?"

Lark nodded even though Tony couldn't see her. She wasn't sure she could speak—the spit in her mouth had dried up. According to her monitors, 20th from Belmont to Stark was teeming with zombies. "Holy crap." Lark managed, gripping the gun controller.

Tony's voice shook through the radio. "I'm going up Belmont and come in from the east—keep an eye on the monitors."

"Yeah." Lark didn't need to be told twice, though Tony

probably would tell her again.

Big Bessie started moving again. Lark understood what Tony was attempting. He was assuming the zombies were only massing from the direction of the waterfront. It was a decent plan—a lot of zombies lurked down around the old warehouses.

Lark barely had time to really ponder what the hell would make the zombies behave this way when a scattering of heat sigs appeared on the screen. The zombies were coming down 28th on a collision course with Big Bessie.

"Incoming. I'm taking them out." Lark advised Tony. She aimed, fired the driver's side guns as they passed 28th. More blips showed up on the screen, and Lark kept up a constant rat-tat of gunfire. Tony turned onto 33rd. More zombies, more shooting. They turned onto Belmont. More zombies. Lark kept shooting. They were about eight blocks from the shiver's place.

For a moment Lark thought Tony's gamble had worked—there were only a few zombies, the normal amount, scattered along Belmont. Most were drifting slowly in the same direction as Big Bessie—towards the shiver's house. Lark kept shooting while watching the monitor. Even blasting every zombie in sight wasn't having the usual effect of relieving her anxiety. She was pretty sure all those brain munchers were heading for the shiver's place. She couldn't say how she knew, just that she was certain down to her bones. Of course the why remained to be answered—she'd heard of zombies swarming in a feeding frenzy, but these zombies weren't frenzied. If anything they were focused, if that was even possible for a brain muncher.

There! Just what she's been dreading—a mass of heat sigs on the monitor and, yep, the red blinking light showing their destination was right in the thick of them.

Tony piped up. "Lark, what do you think we should do?"

Dude must be terrified if he was conceding Lark could have superior knowledge.

"Looks pretty solid on the heat sig." Lark tapped her fingers on the side of the monitor, considering their best move. Not completing the pickup wasn't an option even in this situation. The company guaranteed that the client would be retrieved no matter what. Not for the first time, Lark wished for the fancy helicopters like they had at the L.A. branch. But it was a fact that the L.A. wealthy outnumbered the Portland wealthy, impacting local profit margins and resources.

She shoved those dreams to the same place her dreams of hiking the Pacific Crest Trail lived. *Okay, focus, lots of zombies in a seething mass, surrounding the shiver's home.* Something pinged in her subconscious. Weren't they near…? "Hey Tony, am I crazy or is the shiver holed up in Portland Catholic High?"

Tony gave a short, mirthless laugh. "Yeah, you're crazy, but this isn't a symptom."

"Well, damn. The shiver could be anywhere inside the school building." Lark shot a couple of zombies who meandered by Big Bessie.

"You didn't read the message, did you? The shiv...the client is in the back, in the science labs, off the outdoor basketball courts." Derision over Lark's lack of preparedness seemed to balance Tony, because he sounded calmer.

Lark ignored the tone; it was the driver's job to know such facts, since the driver was the retriever. "Okay, so around back." She pressed a few buttons widening the area the monitor scanned. "Crap, there's just as many in our way. Well, I guess using Big Bessie as a battering ram is our only way in."

"Crap," Tony echoed. "I was afraid you'd say that." He grunted, and Lark heard the distinctive snap of the special webbed harness drivers wore when plowing into a hoard. Lark knew Tony would be checking the doors and windows, confirming all were secure. Lark didn't really like the guy, but she felt a little bad that Tony was at risk while she was relatively safe in the steel box. If everything went as planned, Lark would only unlock the door after Tony had retrieved and scanned the shiver for the zombie virus. Then Lark would open the door just wide enough to yank the guy inside. If, as was becoming likely, things went south and Tony was compromised—the politically correct word for munched—then Lark had to finish the pickup. Her stomach clenched at the thought.

Tony gunned Big Bessie's engine as if ready for a drag race. Big Bessie shot forward at a speed that belied the truck's large size. Lark gripped the gun controller, shooting in every direction. No need to aim, the brain munchers were so thick. Tony yelled as they rammed into the first wave of bodies. Through the monitors, Lark saw bodies exploding from her gunfire, felt the bumps from hitting bodies, and heard the thuds of corpses hitting the truck. Gore, guts, wet splatting sounds. *Thump, slap, bump. Thump, slap, thump*. Zombies don't scream, just make weird grunting sounds. The voiceless carnage continued as Big Bessie muscled her way through until they were in the middle of the basketball court—completely surrounded by zombies, all scrabbling to get inside to eat Tony and Lark's delectable brains.

Tony stopped so suddenly that Lark gasped; they were near the door to the labs.

"Lark." Tony panted as if he'd been running uphill. "I don't see a way to get out of the truck here, not with so many zombies. Looks like there's a sort of foyer area between the door and the labs. I'm going to ram through the door and hope Big Bessie blocks off the zombies while I make the run. Can you to aim to the sides and back and try to keep them off us? Hopefully the client knows we're here."

Lark bit her cheeks, fending off hysterical laughter. "If he doesn't know we're here, then he's deaf."

Banging against Big Bessie's sides continued as Tony

punched the accelerator and managed to find more speed in the truck's engine. He growled over the radio. "Brace for impact."

Lark realigned the guns. Wouldn't do to shoot front. Bad form, killing a customer. Aim for the back and sides. Tony accelerated; Big Bessie plowed through something hard. The door. Lark jerked back and forth in her seat. The truck rocked to a stop, obstructing the hole it had created in the school building's wall.

All was quiet. Until the pounding began at the back of the truck. Through the sounds of beating Lark heard Tony. "You okay?"

"Yeah, you?"

"Yeah." Tony paused and then continued. "Okay, I see our client waving from a window in the lab." His voice trailed off.

"Tony, what's up?" Lark focused one of her cameras towards the lab but the picture wasn't the best and she could only see a vague shape in the lab window.

Tony cleared his throat, gave a short laugh. "Bailey Woodson is, I believe, a she. Mid-sixties, short."

Lark didn't see why that mattered. "Well, go get her." She didn't care if the shiver was a mewling baby; she just wanted to get out of there. There was a beer, check that, many beers, waiting for her in her tiny apartment back at HQ.

"Yes, yes, of course." In the monitor aimed at the driver's seat, Tony's head disappeared and reappeared.

Lark watched as her partner hoisted the AK-47, wearing his protective gloves and helmet. "Right, you know the drill. I go get her, test her, she passes the test, we get back here, and you take her in." Tony swallowed audibly. "We go home."

"Roger that." Lark said fervently. Her palms were sweating, and she wiped them on the slick fabric of her coverall.

Tony huffed out a breath, opened the door and ran like hell through the zombie-free hallway to the lab. Lark focused on killing as many of zombies surrounding the back of the truck as she could. It should have been easy, they were packed in thickly, but they were coming so rapidly that for every one that she killed, two more took its place. She watched the monitor for any blips in Tony's path; a sign that zombies had infiltrated the hallway. So far, no zombies had slipped through to gaps between Big Bessie and the wall. The pounding on the back had become more of a constant thumping, less like a fist hitting the metal and more like whole bodies.

While her eyes and hands focused on killing zombies, Lark kept her ears tuned to the radio where Tony kept up a running monologue.

"Okay, Lark, the shiver is holed up in one of the labs, like we thought. I can see her through the glass. Looks like she normally has metal shutters over them, but she's got the ones near the door open." He paused, and Lark heard gunfire. "Looks like we got an incursion—can you…"

Lark was already shooting the zombies coming down the hallway. Where had they come from?

"Thanks. I'm almost there. Damn, she's equipped—guns around the door, along the walls, the shutters, metal doors. I can see supplies through the window. Not sure why she'd need to leave, really. Weird, she's got a bunch of rats and monkeys in cages."

Lark snorted.

Tony said. "Okay, yeah, but she's really calm. Got a backpack on, just watching me. It's a bit creepy."

Lark didn't see how any shiver could be creepier than the brain munchers surrounding them, but whatever.

Tony announced. "I'm at the door." Lark heard the sound of a fist banging against metal. "Ma'am, can you let me in?"

Lark noticed more zombies coming down the hallway. She aimed; she shot. "Hey Tony, looks like they're getting thick, not sure how they're getting in, but hurry up."

"Yeah. We're on our way, she was all set. Just need to give her the test. Pricking her now."

Lark began the 20 second countdown.

20—Lark rattled off a round of gunfire in the back.

17—Zombies completely filled the basketball court.

15—Lark took out a couple trying to slip past the truck.

13—Lark mowed down about a hundred of them, guessing they'd have to drive over the bodies.

10—For the first time she really worried about running out of ammo.

8—Crap, a whole herd of them was heading down the hallway straight into Tony's path back to the truck.

6—Lark blasted the herd to pieces.

5—Where were they coming from?

4—Lark shoved her hair off her sweaty forehead.

3—More filled the hallway.

2—How were they getting in?

1—

"She's clean." Tony reported.

"Good. We've got a big problem."

"Yeah, I know."

A new voice rang, the shiver's strong, rough tones commanding the situation. "They are coming in from the gym. Sorry about that, folks. I know this is a tough one. The zombies clearly have an affinity for me." That was new, a shiver acknowledging the difficulties in retrieval. "I've got an idea. You, in the truck, you're not allowed to leave unless your partner is compromised, correct?"

"Yeah, I mean, yes ma'am." Lark resisted the urge to salute. Who was this lady, this Bailey Johnson?

"Glad to know Steve is still using the protocol we set up." Lark was shocked to hear the woman refer to ZARA's CEO so casually. Before she could comment, Bailey continued. "Here's the plan: you in the truck, lay down suppressing fire along your left while this young man and I run like hell for the truck."

Pretty obvious plan, but Lark didn't argue—just started shooting. Over the noise of gunfire, she heard

Tony and Bailey breathing heavily as they ran.

Tony gasped out. "Almost there."

Lark started to cheer, but the sound died in her throat. Zombies were coming around Big Bessie on the driver's side. In her focus on the hallway, Lark had lost track of the zombies in the court. "Tony, Tony, watch out, on your right."

Lark jerked when Tony screamed and Bailey swore. The truck rocked, and through the camera aimed at the driver's seat Lark saw Tony's hand grasping for the steering wheel only to be yanked away. She gripped the gun controller but was unable to shoot into the mass for fear of hitting Tony and Bailey. It looked like the zombies weren't attacking Bailey—more oddness. Even though Tony was wearing his protective gear, it was mostly a delay of the inevitable in a horde. Zombies were really good at finding exposed skin when given enough time.

Tony's screams ended in a horrible gurgle. Lark froze when the shiver, Bailey, snapped at her over the radio. "Let me in. Now!"

Lark pulled herself together enough to see she was in the cab, perched on the side of the passenger's seat. She was tiny, elf-like, with short hair and bright eyes. Her eyes focused on the camera as she spoke to her.

Lark swallowed, she really hated this part so freakin' much. "You might be bit. I gotta come out and test you again first." Her bowels threatened to betray her, but she forced himself to clench. Her subconscious and, frankly, her conscious screamed at her not to go out. They were completely surrounded, and Big Bessie rocked like two teenagers were making out in the back. But if Bailey was bit and Lark let her into the back, she was risking her own death. If she left Bailey in the cab to fend for herself, Lark was dead for sure because the company would come after her. It was best to follow procedure—test the shiver again then, if she wasn't infected, let her in back so they could call for help.

"Okay, hurry up then." Bailey spoke briskly, shifting out of the way of the door.

Lark didn't let herself think; she just opened the door and kneeled in the spot Bailey had just vacated. She left the door open but blocked the entrance with her body. Bailey held out her arm, and Lark pricked it just below the elbow, mentally beginning the count as the horde howled outside the truck. They didn't speak; both stared at her arm, waiting for the betraying bumps to appear.

Ten seconds left. So far her skin was clear; Lark realized she was holding her breath, and she let it out slowly, almost swallowing her tongue when the crash of breaking glass sounded from the driver's seat window. Training took over, and she jumped in front of the shiver, throwing up her arm in automatic defense of the attacking zombie. Too late, she realized she'd forgotten her protective gloves as the gripping teeth from a zombie clamped down on her wrist.

Lark screamed in fury and fear. She jerked her arm

away, horrified as her skin tore off; left hanging from the creature's rotting lips. Stupid, stupid, not to be holding a gun or a knife. More zombies tried forced their way into the cab, fighting to get past the zombie blocking the narrow opening.

"Not again!" Bailey sounded more annoyed than afraid. "Come on."

Lark was in shock. She felt her thoughts, her memories, what made her who she was, draining from her mind. She retained enough awareness to know Bailey quickly climbed over her body into the back of the truck. She thought, *Good she'll lock herself in and wait for help.* When Bailey grabbed Lark's shaking body under her arms and started hauling her into the back, Lark tried to pull away. "No, no." Was the old lady crazy?

"Come on. It'll be ok." Bailey shushed her.

Was the shiver stupid? Any minute now Lark would Z-out and start attacking. Jesus, the lady was strong though. Bailey dragged her to the side of the truck, pulled Lark's unresisting arms up and locked them into the cuffs designed to hold zombies caught for testing—the kind of pickup Lark had never done or wanted to do.

All the while Bailey muttered. "It'll be okay. This is a good spot of luck for you. It'll be okay. You're lucky." Was she talking to Lark? Lark no longer seemed to have the power of speech to ask, her tongue felt thick. "You'll be—"

The woman's words faded into gibberish. Lark's mind

went black along with the world around her; her last aware thought was "ouch" when a sharp stab went up her arm.

Thud! Lark jerked forward, only stopping because of the chains holding her arms. Blinking against the light, she stared around.

She was still in the truck, zombies still raged outside, and Bailey sat in the gunner's seat holding a rifle watching her avidly. Lark's thoughts were clear again, she knew himself, and she didn't want to eat anyone's brains. Her mouth was dry, roughening her words. "What," she cleared her throat, "happened?"

Bailey smiled, looking like a happy elf. "Welcome back."

"What happened?" Lark rattled her chains. "I was bitten, I was Z-ing out. No one comes back from that."

Bailey got up, set the rifle down and walked over to take her pulse. With a satisfied nod of her head, she began unlocking the cuffs. Lark tried to pull away, but she put a gentle hand on her shoulder. "Congratulations, you're the first human to be cured of the zombie virus."

Lark gaped at her while Bailey finished removing the cuff and pushed the chains aside. Lark didn't move. "No one has a cure. There isn't a cure." She reached for the chains and cuffs, intending to put them back on.

Bailey sighed, sitting back on her heels. "No one until now."

"Who are you?" Lark was afraid to stand, afraid it was

a dream brought on by Z-ing out. Any minute it would fade, and she would be out there mindlessly shuffling and chomping.

Bailey settled back with a bitter smile. "I'm one of the people who created this whole mess. We were trying to find a cure for mad cow disease and it all went wrong." She winced when Lark surged to her feet. "Yes, I understand you're angry. It seems only right I find the cure—which is why I called for pickup. I just wish it hadn't taken me ten years. I had to hide out; people were trying to kill me. I managed to set up a lab here, though it wasn't easy." She frowned at the walls around them vibrating with zombie fists. "I think they know, the zombies. Not sure how, but more have congregated here in the past day."

Lark didn't care anymore why the brain munchers were so thick here. She was still reeling from Bailey's announcement. The shiver was the architect of the horror they'd been living with of the past ten years? She should throw Bailey outside with her creations. From Bailey's expression, she knew what Lark was thinking, but she didn't move. Just watched Lark with a wary yet wry expression.

Lark stepped forward, grabbed Bailey's arm, and dragged her to her feet. She reached for the door handle, the action causing her torn sleeve to fall away from her arm. Her wrist was still bleeding from the zombie bite, the impression of teeth marring her skin. But her head was clear, and she knew she was okay, just like she'd been promised. She was still human because of this woman. She met Bailey's eyes. "You have a cure? For all zombies?"

"Yes. Before I used it on you I tested a few zombies. They were cured of being zombies but sadly too far gone physically to live much longer. If I'd had a better lab, I could have helped them more." Bailey kept her gaze on Lark. "Once I get it to the labs at ZARA, we can begin making more, enough to get started."

Lark blew out her breath, let go of Bailey's arm, and picked up the panic button. "Well then, let's get out of this crap so you can save the world." She kept her eyes on Bailey's as she radioed. "HQ, I've got a two-person emergency pickup. Send reinforcements. Now!"

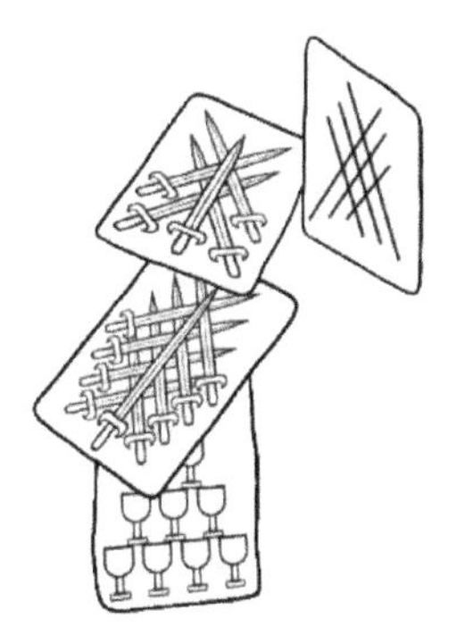

Misreadings

Tonya Lippert

At an alleyway tea house, Clare sits at a low wooden table and stares at a spread of tarot cards, face down. Old yearnings surface. Yearnings for answers, for hope, for certainty.

The reader, an older man who has traveled extensively through India, says he'll come back when Clare's ready. He instructs her to repeat a specific question for the cards and then mix them into one deck. The single deck will be his cue to return.

Clare sighs. She has questions about her lover Michael's fidelity and the futility of continuing to hope one day he might maybe actually love her.

But she knows from experience that yes-no questions tend to be the wrong ones for invisible forces. She'd tried readers of all kinds as a college student. Card readers, palm readers, psychics and once, when she'd gone to New Orleans for Mardi Gras, a voodoo priestess who'd thrown sticks. Or was it bones?

During another spell, for over a year, she'd driven to Venice Beach every few months for a reading under the umbrella of an older woman with a leaning-toward glamour who almost hit the mark. At least her large blonde hair and layers of makeup made her easy to spot. But it was her air of certainty that appealed to Clare. It meant that Clare could choose from her well-worn cards with faith.

Clare's now unable to remember anything her trusted reader said, let alone whether any of it came true. As far as she knows, none of it came untrue. There's the rub. Clare knows of only two times when any reader had been wrong—one was the priestess—and these unfulfilled predictions were easy to disprove.

And there was the one time she'd had proof of extraordinary forces. She'd been describing a scene from *The Evil Dead* to an ex-boyfriend while they were driving.

"Two of the friends staying at the cabin have a deck of cards," Clare said. "One flips the cards while the other guesses what's on them. She gets them all wrong, but her friend pretends she's getting them all right. Suddenly, another girl, facing away, begins calling the cards out, getting them all right for real. As she keeps calling out, her voice becomes deeper and more disturbing, until she gets to the last card: Jack of Clubs."

Clare had imitated the voice of the girl from the movie as her ex-boyfriend parked the car.

Stepping out and shutting the car door, Clare'd noticed something under her shoe: a playing card, about a quarter of the usual size. She picked it up. *Jack of Clubs*. Clare kept the card for good luck. Years later, she lost it.

Clare thought she was over this magical and mystical shit. It's all karma, really. What we do has consequences. Does she need them pointed out to her? Guess so, because here she is once again yielding to the call of the cards, tempted by their promise of certainty because the uncertainty is killing her.

Staring at the unfamiliar pattern on the cards before her, Clare formulates her question. *What's really going on between me and Michael?* No, the question's inadequate. *What's really going on between me and Michael now and later?* Still inadequate. *What's really going on between and me and Michael now and later, including any other woman or women he's having sex with?* She hopes the question closes any loopholes.

Clare envisions the kind of reading she'd like but knows she's unlikely to receive:

"This one says someone close is deceiving you."

"Close how?" she asks to eliminate room for doubt.

"A lover. Your present lover."

"No!" she cries inside herself.

Clare plays the fantasy out further as she sips her Chai, savoring the heat of temperature and spice on her tongue and lips. What if the cards say Michael is deceiving her? Will she believe it? Will she believe it if they say there is no deceit? And what about the possibility her lover could start deceiving her at any time? Will the cards say no deceit now and no deceit later?

And then there's the companion question, if the cards say he's deceiving her: What to do? Will the cards give her direction? *"This card says you need to find another lover."* Except Clare has no desire to get over one lover by getting under another.

It's time. Clare focuses on her question. The reader said to repeat it at least three times. Just to be clear to the forces penetrating the cards, Clare asks about nine. Then she stacks the cards together and watches the reader sit down across from her.

"The first card will show the core of your question," he says.

Clare nods. He turns it over. Six of Wands. *Victory.* Clare exhales. Seems like a good start.

"This is the card of clarity," the reader says. "Whatever goal you are applying yourself to, you have clarity about your intentions and desires. If you keep doing what's been working within the situation, you will achieve your goal." Then he adds, "Whether the clarity is to continue pursuing the goal, give up on it, or adjust."

He's covering all the bases. If I have clarity, why am I getting a reading? Clare keeps an open mind.

The reader tells Clare she now has a choice.

Choice one, a card to the left of the first that shows her past and a card to the right that shows her future. Choice two, a card to the right that reveals what she is or could be doing that is 'helpful' and a card to the left that shows what is or could be 'not helpful.'

Clare picks choice number two. She'd already lived her past, so why hear about it?

The reader starts with what's helpful. He flips over the Five of Swords. *Defeat.*

Well, this is interesting, Clare thinks. *Victory and Defeat side by side.*

The reader says, "This card is about facing the final obstacle to getting what you want. It's the thing to overcome, the thing to confront that will clear the way to your goal. Again," he says, covering all the bases, "it could also mean leaving the situation, if this is the clarity represented by the first card."

"Here's what's not helpful in the situation," the reader continues as he lays down card number three: Nine of Swords. *Cruelty.*

Clare straightens up. Saying, "Fuck it," and abandoning whatever it is Clare's question pertains to would be 'not helpful.'

"The card is about starting over, which, given its position, is unlikely to work." Finally, a more specific answer, albeit surprising.

The reader points to *Defeat* on the other side and says, "The third card says no to merely leaving the situation as the helpful path."

Clare's thankful the reader offers one more card to go

above the first. He says it can reveal the future of the situation or expand on what her clarity is about. At this point, Clare's afraid to mess with the future by knowing it.

"Expand," she says.

Ten of Cups. *Satiety*. It means the clarity is about her heart, about desire. A new desire. Something new has gotten her heart excited.

Clare leaves the tea house twenty dollars short and a little more hopeful. Certainty probably costs a lot more than hope, she figures.

Still, she will apply certainty. The reader said to apply what had been working with the relationship. Certainty had. Or at least, turning toward trust that her lover would see her value, and she only needed to act as if she were certain of this to get it to happen. Actions have consequences. Karma.

A few days later, she has the chance to test out this idea. She had bought tickets for her and Michael to go to a comedy show. He'd confirmed he'd be there before she bought the tickets, days prior to the event, and the day of. Clare'd needed the confirmations because the one thing she could count on with Michael was being unable to count on him. She was action; he was words.

Two hours before the show he texts her: *Would you hate me if I asked for a rain check?* Clare texts back that she'd be really disappointed.

When her lover calls soon after, Clare pauses. She

wants to sound upbeat and confident instead of angry and desperate. Before answering the phone, she inhales and exhales and says to herself, "Yes, he will come."

When her lover says his sister needs help with something, Clare suggests he could come for just the headliner's one-hour set and still have time to help his sister with whatever she needed. It had to do with his sister's lover coming to town. Clare imagined it was something easily solved without Michael—a ride from the airport—but she said nothing.

"I'll let you know either way within thirty minutes," he says.

Clare starts her yoga class, repeating, "He's going, he's going."

His text comes during yoga: *Sorry, hun*.

Clare resists giving up on him right then and there. Her reading had advised against abandonment. For the next two days, she continues to resist as Michael texts her about his back hurting from soccer, about his socializing, and he says nothing about the rain check, nothing about seeing her.

Clare sends one-liner responses to his texts: *Wow. Oh, interesting*. They reveal none of her torment.

Clare feels as if she's leaving the relationship the way she used to sneak out of bed to avoid waking her grandfather. Scoot to the edge of the bed. Wait. One leg off the side. Wait. Other leg down. Wait. Slide down until one hand and then the other touches carpet. Wait. Crawl out of the room, listening for movement. Open the door slowly. Shift body out. Close the door soundlessly. Run.

As Michael's texts get longer and hers shorter, Clare finds clarity. She emails Michael. He might expect an email begging for his time—arrogant fuck—but she'd learned. She'd already told him she needed more time with him, more time than once every two to three weeks. Each time, he'd strung her along. "I can see you once a week. I could even see you twice a week." Never happened. "I'll try to do better." Nothing changed.

Instead of begging for more, she asks for less. Less texting. Clare requests that Michael stop texting her unless it is to say he wants to see her. She's tired of this relationship by text with the occasional sex and time out and about.

About twelve hours after her email, Michael is with her. Predictable. Each time she loosens her hold, he tightens his. Only, it's the briefest visit she's ever had with him. Just under two hours, and he wants to go nowhere. Except to her bed.

Several lonely nights pass, and Clare wakes to a banging at her window. Her outside shutter, half-raised, knocks into the glass with each gust of wind. She checks her phone for the time. 4:00 a.m. Without wanting or expecting it, she sees '*Michael*' and a couple of paragraphs of text. He never texts paragraphs.

She feels a sinking inside her chest down to her abdomen. Her last text had been, *Wow, you were up late,* after he'd texted her at 1:30 a.m. the night before.

Must be a break-up text. Maybe a confession that yeah, he was up late because he was with somebody else, and so, well, it's a good time to end things.

Clare falls back to sleep. At least she'll have certainty. There'll be no relationship. No more questions about what to do.

When she wakes up a few hours later, Clare discovers that Michael's text says only, *Yes, I had a long night, sweet dreams*. The paragraphs are from somebody else. She must have touched her screen when she picked up her phone, switching from Michael's text to the other's.

The relief and gratitude Clare feels are unexpected. She's sure unseen forces are preventing her and Michael from parting ways. It strikes her how people can act as if extraordinary things were ordinary and as if ordinary things were extraordinary. People seemed poorly designed to respond to the extraordinary.

Clare has this on her mind when, two weeks later, she finally has confirmation of her lover's deceit. The worst kind of confirmation except for its certainty.

He'd said she was the only one. He'd agreed they'd keep each other safe. He'd been her only one. She'd kept him safe.

Now she has herpes.

When Clare confronts Michael, he says she should have known better and insisted on a condom. He gets hit on all the time. Does she know how hard it is to constantly say no? So, yeah, he's sleeping with a couple other women, and now he has herpes. He also just found out and, if it helps her feel better, he's mortified. But, it's her fault, too, for being so careless. Hardly anybody's really monogamous anymore. It's old-fashioned.

"I trusted you."

"Sorry, hun."

When he leaves, Clare thinks of the anime *Death Note*. Michael's lucky she has no book of death to write his name into. And even if she had one, she'd still need something to stop her feelings.The feelings of loss, of anger. She needed something to erase her thoughts of being spoiled and then discarded, of being a fool.

Days later, Clare realizes no invisible forces will help her with this one. Michael will go on lying to other women, using them the way he used her. When she texts him that herpes is forever, he says she needs to move on, the way he already had.

Certainty washes over her. Clare calls Michael over for one last time together. After all, the damage has already been done. Maybe they can at least have a memorable goodbye. He agrees.

Later, as candles bring light to the dark, Clare feels Michael's ejaculate slide down her inner thighs right before she slips into her hot bath. She closes her eyes to breathe the steam into her body. She feels nothing. Nothing except the hot water against her body. Nothing except the stickiness of Michael's blood where the water has yet to draw it away.

He'd trusted her. Never expected any of it. In one night, she executed karma and her lover. And all she'd needed to get what she wanted was her own two hands and an ordinary object. Sharp, but ordinary. Call her old-fashioned.

She moves the bloody water around with her hand and giggles. "Sorry, hun."

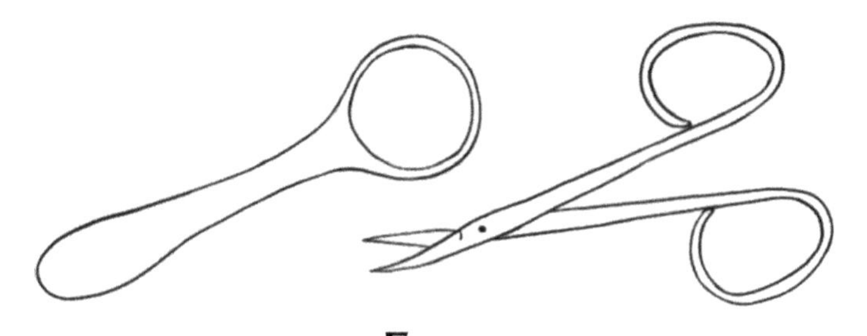

Eyes

Heather S. Ransom

I eased the spoon down into the baby's eye socket until the suction sound turned to a soft *pop*. After clipping the optical nerve, I started on the other eye. One down, one to go. I had to reposition the spoon when it didn't slide in smoothly. Adjusting my grip on the handle, I pushed down harder this time, thinking that, although it technically wasn't a "spoon," I could have eaten cereal with it.

"Put on some speed, Zif." A foot tapped impatiently. Fen never could stand still.

"I'm on it. We should have broken in to do this last week."

Fen snorted. "Three sets in seven months. Hope these last a little longer."

Finally, another audible pop. A firm snip, then carefully, I dropped both eyes in the quick fix jar, and pulled a crimper out of my pocket.

"Hey, you can't blame me for tossing that second set.

Dealers who sell unmatched eyes should be put down." I'd felt crazy with those eyes. It was hard enough keeping check on one set of urges.

My life was tough, but it was mine. At least I hadn't been born a stock baby, shunted after harvesting. I glanced across the other babies available, hoping I'd made a good choice. I mean, it was impossible to tell. They all pretty much looked the same. I could deal with the urges; I was just hoping for a little more time. We all knew that stealing a new set from a private stock lab carried huge risks.

Those designated as "permanently sighted" didn't know how good they had it. They just put in a call and a new set was delivered to their door. They never had to harvest their own. But I needed these eyes.

I crimped the nerve endings with new adapters. A burnt, slightly metallic smell filled the air. That was a good sign.

"Any day." The foot tapping started again.

I popped my bad eye out first. It hurt some, but I was used to it by now. And, once your sight started to go, the nerves didn't work right anyway. The virus had infected it about a month ago, so it was pretty much already dead. I felt along the optic nerve to find the old inset point, cut just behind it, then crimped the new one in. I had sixty seconds to get the other one done. If both eyes weren't connected by then, there'd be a possibility I'd see double for the span of this set. I'd known a guy who'd gone crazy, ripping his out before they even went bad because of double-vision headaches. What a waste.

I let the new eye dangle wet against my cheek. One more pop and crimp. This time completely by touch. That was the scary part of all this. I hated the blind times. They were suffocating.

Taking a deep breath, I gently pulled back my eyelids, one at a time, and softly pushed until the new eyes popped into place. Blinking, I waited for my sight to return.

"Well, how are they?" I heard Fen's footsteps come toward me. "Pretty sweet. Cool green. Good choice on color."

Suddenly a piercing wail filled the room. *The baby!* It was screaming now at the top of its lungs. It shouldn't have done that. *Stock babies don't make noise…unless…*

Fen and I looked at each other astonished.

"Oh my god, you hit the mother lode!" Fen yelled over the top of the shrieking howl. "We've got to get out of here now! They'll kill you to get those eyes!"

The baby came into focus with black, gaping holes where its eyes had been. Its arms flew in random, jerking movements.

I just stood there. Everything seemed in slow motion. The realization of what was happening slowly washed over me. I looked up as Fen grabbed my arm.

"We have to go! Now!" Fen began to drag me across the room. Then a siren added its squealing, and I snapped into action.

I dove after Fen into a small air duct at the back of the room, scrambling for what seemed like forever until we rolled out into a waste pond behind the facility. Glancing back as we started to run for the trees, I saw officers with guns filing out of the building.

Fen's breathing was jagged as we finally slowed to a jog, weaving through the thick brush. "Somebody's going to be…in big trouble. Just think…they had an immune there and…didn't even know it. They should have been…harvesting sooner."

That's when I felt it, so strong and burning. Overwhelming. There's always urges with new eyes since they're connected to the soul of the previous owner, of who they'll become. Mother Teresa, Hitler, or some schmuck in between.

I looked at Fen. Rippling muscles. Smooth skin. My best friend. And I felt for the knife in my pocket.

The blade felt sweet sliding through Fen's throat. No sound came from the open mouth. Wasted. Maybe I should've taken my new eyes out. Tossed them.

But they were immune. Not eyes that you'd give up.

Fen would've understood. A girl's gotta make her own way in this world.

The Old Ways

M.K. Martin

"Rome was the world's most powerful empire. At its height, it even reached our shores. I hope all of you take time, when we stop in Bowness-on-Solway, to see the end of the Roman Wall. Imagine how different Britain would be if the sun had never set on the Roman Empire." The tour guide bubbled on like a runaway stream after a heavy downpour. Deitra leaned her head against the cool glass of the bus window as it finally pulled into the Twisted Tree Inn parking lot. Outside it was raining. Again. Ever since she'd arrived, it had rained.

Somehow, the travel agent had convinced Deitra all those rainy scenes took place during the spring. The rest of the time it's so lovely, the woman had cooed. Lovely, indeed!

Lovely, like her relationship with Jerrold. She sighed. She'd come to England to get over him, not spend the whole trip pining.

Still, it was hard to just put him out of her mind. She'd thought he was The One, her Mr. Right. They'd met when he was at his family's summerhouse near Nag's Head. She'd dropped out of college, moved back home, and resigned herself to a Cinderella life of waitressing at her family's restaurant when Jerrold had shown up and swept her off her feet.

Their dating had been a blur of D.C.'s finest galleries, museums, restaurants, wineries, plays, and concerts. Soon Jerrold asked her to move in. Life was perfect! She had planned her response when he popped the question, planned their wedding, followed by an English honeymoon. She quietly set aside money and gathered travel brochures.

As it turned out, Deitra wasn't the only one quietly working on a project. Jerrold's project was Tiffany, a work colleague. Deitra had met her at a few parties and plays. Jerrold met her at hotels. When Deitra found the receipts, he didn't bother to lie. It was better she knew, he'd said. They were tired of hiding. She moved back home that night.

On her mother's advice, she'd taken this honeymoon trip sans Jerrold.

She hadn't anticipated the constant rain or that her bus tour would be made up of nothing but happy couples. By day four, she hated England.

"...a quaint, charming little inn and pub. I have everyone's room keys." The guide held up a large, ancient brass key. It looked like a prop in a documentary on Merry Ole England.

To an optimistic person, the inn was quaint, even charming. It was definitely old. The Romans had built the original structure over a pagan barrow to claim the land and make a statement. Over the centuries, the rest of the inn had grown around the Roman building. The end result was an architectural crazy quilt of various designs, all sagging toward the low midsection, the pub itself.

Inside smelled of pipe smoke, spilled ale, old polish, and some indefinable but distinct odor Deitra could only think of as 'long history.' A comforting fire snapped and crackled in the wide native stone hearth, located against one wall of the pub. A small stage of ancient planks, shiny from years of scrubbing, sanding, and thousands of feet, nestled against the wall opposite the hearth.

After a bath and a change of clothes, Deitra rejoined the tour group in the pub. She found a lonely perch at the bar, atop a wide, old oaken stool and ordered a pork pie and a pint.

"Do you like this?"

Deitra jumped. A boyishly handsome man had slid onto the stool next to hers. His hair was a short, sandy blonde bristle. He wore a leather jacket that looked both casual and expensive. His dimpled smile was cocksure and reminded her too much of Jerrold. As if any woman was his to claim. Deitra glared at him and focused on her pie.

"*Scusi,* so sorry, my English...I am hoping you are not angry, *bella,*" the blonde man said. His Italian accent, like warm honey, caressed her ears. His face was a picture of sincerity. Deitra felt embarrassed. Poor guy. Not every man was Jerrold.

"No, it's fine. Sorry. I'm just tired," she said.

"Vittore Romano, *incantato.*" He offered a warm, smooth hand.

"I'm Deitra." She shook. "Pleased to meet you." He smiled, his blue eyes direct and a bit too intimate. *Stop that! He's Italian, they're like that. Don't be the ugly American,* she admonished herself. "So," she said, "um, are you here on vacation?" *Idiot! Obviously.*

"Business." His face hardened a little, his eye scanning the room, then back to her. "But not tonight, I think."

"Oh." Deitra toyed with her food.

"Sorry," Vittore said. "This rain, this food, this place it's..." He searched for words then stuck out his tongue and wrinkled his nose.

"Exactly." Deitra smiled.

Vittore chuckled. "Why have you traveled so far for so little?" He waved at the pub. With a hot meal, a cold pint and a roaring fire, the pub seemed homier. Overhead, the old boards creaked and groaned softly, the wind sighing through the numerous eaves. Outside darkness had fallen, and the rain gently drummed on the roof. All things considered, England didn't seem quite as wretched anymore.

"It's more what I was traveling from than to," she said. "A great big from."

Vittore gave her the uncomprehending, hopeful smile common to travelers across every land; the one that says, "I have no idea what you're saying, but go on."

The door crashed open. Wind and rain blew in, sending a soggy chill through the pub. Every head turned to stare at the three dripping figures in the doorway. At first, Deitra wasn't sure who the strangers might be, but as they peeled off their outer layers, she realized they were musicians.

First in the door was a large ruddy man, a dark woolen watch cap snugged down on his head. Between the hat and his enormously fluffy dark red beard, it was hard to make out any facial features apart from the flash of a broad grin and the twinkle of dark eyes. He had a battered guitar case stuffed under his peacoat. A petite, dark haired woman, dressed in a bright red blouse and swirling peasant skirts, followed the redhead in. She carried a flute case and a small flat drum wrapped in waterproof cloth. The last member of the group paused in the door.

For an instant, as the flickering light of the hearth fire hit his eyes, Deitra could have sworn they glowed, flashing gold. She gasped, and Vittore followed her gaze. The stranger stepped into the room. Unlike his companions, he did not rush in out of the wet. His long, dark hair was mostly pushed back, although a few wild strands hung forward, tickling his high cheekbones. The dark man's eyes swept the room, cautious, watchful.

When his eyes met Vittore's, both men stiffened. A slow smile spread across Vittore's face. The dark man nodded a curt salute. He produced a fiddle seemingly out of nowhere and sauntered across to join his fellows. His movements were powerful, yet graceful. He reminded Deitra of panthers she'd seen at the zoo, prowling their enclosures, dreaming their wild, bloody dreams.

The dark-haired woman pulled three chairs up on stage, the silver bangles on her arms tinkling as she moved. The trio spent a few minutes ensuring their instruments had taken no hurt from the damp and then tuning up. The big redheaded man took a position with a foot on one of the chairs, balancing his guitar with its strangely fat bottom across his knee. If Deitra remembered correctly, that was called a bouzouki. The dark-haired woman sat down, arranged her shirts, lifted the small drum, the bohdran, and smiled warmly at the audience.

The dark stranger strode to the edge of the stage and stood, thumbs hooked in the pockets of his worn jeans. He said nothing, his bright eyes dancing over the room. A hush fell as, one by one, people met his gaze. Still, he said nothing. Deitra found herself holding her breath.

Suddenly, the dark stranger's face broke into an impish grin.

"That's right," he said, his voice rich and low, pitched

to catch each ear personally. "We're back. I know some a yous and for the rest, get ready to dance. I'm Brayden. I lead this merry band. Salix." The woman waved. "And Fáthach," The large man nodded.

"We are Tuatha Dé Danann." He bowed dramatically, then swept up, the fiddle already in the crook of his neck.

The music burst to life with a nearly impossible wail from the fiddle, joined by the drum, and held together by the melody of the bouzouki. The tune was a wild reel, each round moving faster and faster seeming on the verge of collapsing into chaotic madness, but always returning to the core melody, a deeply stirring sound. It was like a storm, a whirlwind of sound rising, building, crashing and then, with one final mighty flourish of the fiddle, it stopped.

No one moved. No one even breathed. Slowly, Brayden opened his eyes. For just an instant, Deitra again saw the flash of gold as if his eyes burned with mystical inner fire.

"*Sláinte!*" cried the bartender, raising his mug to the musicians. The crowd burst into raucous applause. A grinning waitress hurried over with a tray of drinks. "On the house," she said.

Brayden squatted down, so they were face to face. "*Go raibh maith agat,*" he murmured, his voice just on the decent side of 'in public'. Straightening, he held his mug aloft. "To yous, good people the lot!" He winked at the waitress. "And to women who know how to make a man smile." The waitress blushed and scurried for the safety of the bar. Deitra wished she were a waitress.

"Cretins," muttered Vittore.

"You don't like the local color?" Deitra asked, eyebrow raised.

"Pale shadows." He waved dismissively as the little band struck up a soft, lamenting ballad. Brayden's singing voice was every bit as enchanting as his speaking voice, low, deep, steady and thrilling—thrilling in ways Jerrold had never thrilled her.

"Their time is long past, and see! They dance on. They should give up, admit defeat with dignity," Vittore said.

"Umm, it's a band," Deitra said. "Not a war."

"*Certo.*" Vittore nodded reluctantly. "Of course. The lady is right. Come." He held out a hand. "Let's get away from this...how do you say? Racket, yes?"

Deitra looked up, meeting his beautiful blue eyes, his boyish smile. So sure all he had to do was hold out his hand and she'd swoon into his arms.

She'd made her share of mistakes, from dropping out of school to moving to D.C. Probably coming to England, too.

She looked into Vittore's eyes and saw another mistake waiting.

"I'm fine here," Deitra said.

A frown creased Vittore's brow. "*Scusi*. You didn't understand. Is no problem. We will have dinner in the restaurant. This," he shot a dark look at the band, "is not a place for such a *belladonna*." He took her by the arm to escort her into the small, adjacent dining area.

"No." Deitra wrenched her arm away more forcefully than she intended. She could see the shock, the slow comprehension. It felt good, powerful.

"I'll stay. Thanks." She turned away from him, back to the stage. Brayden's eyes were on her. He inclined his head to her gravely, but his eyes twinkled. It wasn't her imagination. His eyes were golden.

Deitra ignored the rustle of cloth, the quick, angry stomping of feet as Vittore departed. She focused on the band. Several of the tour group couples were dancing. They looked awkward and silly, their bright American clothes standing out like disoriented tropical birds in Antarctica, but they were having a marvelous time. Whenever someone seemed to flag or become self-conscious, Brayden's eyes were on them, encouraging them, urging them on, making it all right to let go, to just dance.

"Miss?" The bartender held out a hand.

Deitra gulped down the rest of her beer and took the man's rough, weathered hand. "Why the hell not?" She hopped off the stool, lost her footing, and fell laughing into the bartender's arms.

"Steady on, miss," he said. "Had a wee bit too much, then?"

"Nah," Deitra giggled. "I'm fine. Dance me!" The bartender chuckled and spun her out onto the floor. She had no idea what she was doing. It didn't matter.

She twirled and whirled from one partner to the next and drank several pints of dark, bitter beer. Somewhere among the jigs, the stathspeys, waltzes, and reels, Deitra forgot that she hated Britain, forgot that she was the lone lonely heart in a tour group full of lovey-dovey couples. She forgot the sting of Jerrold's smug face when she handed back her keys to his apartment.

It seemed only moments later when Deitra found herself outside. Rather than seeming soggy and depressing, the chilly night air revived her. The wind rattled through the trees, sending spatters of rain down. Overhead, the dissipating clouds scudded across the sky. The moon, a silvery blue orb, nestled low in the hills, as if it too were exhausted by a night of dancing.

Deitra lifted loose strands of sweaty hair from her neck. She shuddered at the cold wind's kiss, goosebumps rising up along her arms. A mist was rolling in from the sea. Its ghostly white fingers reached into every hollow and nook, sliding along the low ground, filling it, enfolding the world in white.

"You know, they say on nights like this, the fey can come through the mists."

Deitra jumped. She hadn't even heard the heavy door swing on its ancient hinges.

Brayden stood next to her, his pale skin seeming to glow in the faint moonlight—a stark contrast to his dark hair and bright gold eyes. He smiled wistful. "They say once the fey ruled all these lands. They were so full o' life then. Wise animals, ancient trees, less rain." He winked at her.

"Fey, like fairies?" Deitra asked. *Stupid question!* But Brayden didn't laugh, didn't even smirk.

"A bit. Fairies, wee flying folk, they're pixies. Nah, fey are like..." He searched for words. "What you call elves, then. Taller than men and fair. All sorts 'a mysteries in these isles even still. They never could drive out all magic." He stared down toward the sea. His bright eyes searched the darkness, almost as if he expected something to come out of the mists. As if he longed for it.

Up close, he was even more captivating. The wind ruffled his dark hair, tugging at loose strands to play along the curve of his neck, his strong jaw. His lips were full and inviting. Kissable lips. *Kissable? Stop acting like a drunk groupie!*

Deitra tore her eyes from his handsome face to follow his gaze. She half expected to see something moving in the mist, half expected to see...what? A fey? She giggled at the thought. Brayden turned back to her, a smile on his face but lacking its earlier spark. The show smile of the consummate performer. She could see in his eyes the flash of disappointment, resignation.

"Come on then," he said. "Some say it's bad luck to be out alone on Samhain."

"Samhain?" Deitra echoed.

"In America, Halloween, ya?" Brayden tipped his head

at the wispy clouds and thickening mist. "The dead return to settle themselves, to say farewell 'afore moving along. That's why we came, then. Tonight, the doors between here and there are open."

"Huh?" She couldn't make sense of his words. Maybe she was too drunk. *Or maybe he's not making sense,* she thought. She didn't care if he made sense or not. His voice was gentle, patient, yet strong and sure. He didn't treat her like she was stupid because she didn't understand. Encouraged, she pressed on. "Like ghosts?"

"Aye, ghosts, fetches, wraiths, haunts, geists, all of them." Brayden grinned, the mischievous spark back in his eye. "D'you want to see 'em?"

Deitra grinned back gamely. "Sure, okay. Show me your scary ghosts."

"Right." Brayden stuck out a strong, calloused hand. "Brayden," he said.

"I know," Deitra said. "I saw you come in."

"I know," he said. "I saw you." He let the thought hang between them, and she hung a hundred wild implications on it.

"D'you have a name or should I just call you a store?"

"A store?"

He laughed, a completely unselfconscious sound. Deitra's heart surged. She longed to make him laugh again.

"No, not a store, silly girl. *A stòr*. It means 'precious'."

"Deitra's fine." She ducked her head, hoping he'd

chalk the bloom in her cheeks to the drink.

"Deitra." He rolled her name. God, but she loved his lilting accent.

"That's a fine, old name," Brayden said.

He led the way around the inn. Deitra let herself be guided through a world of fog and indistinct shadows, descending a winding goat trail, her heart hammering. Below, the sound of crashing surf echoed, booming against the cliffs, reverberating through sea caves. The scents of the cold waters of the Irish Sea, salt, and fish mingled with the scents of heather, damp earth, dead leaves, and wood smoke from the inn.

Deitra shivered with cold. She was ready to return to the warm safety of the inn when Brayden stopped. Deitra stumbled and he steadied her easily. He tipped his chin towards a large lumpy shape, rising out of the fog, like the prow of a ghost ship.

"A cairn," Brayden said. His voice low and reverent, breath warm against her neck. Again, goosebumps prickled her arms, but not from the temperature. Deitra took a deep breath and stepped forward. The stacked rocks seemed to float, an island in a sea of rolling mist. A stone wall ringed the graveyard, an empty archway provided access. Worn headstones marked the graves of the long dead. Ahead, barely outlined by the dim moonlight, the remains of a small, tumbled down church hunkered at the far edge of the graveyard.

From inside the church, a light flared. Brayden

stiffened, his grip on her hand tightening.

"Finally found the courage and ventured from your hole?" said a familiar voice. Vittore stood in the doorway of the church, his face illuminated by the orange glow of his cigarette. He smiled contemptuously at Brayden.

"Why tonight, Roman?" Brayden asked. His voice sounded breezy, casual; his posture was anything but. He was poised to strike, tightly coiled. Again, Deitra could see the wildness in him, the restrained power.

"Why not?" Vittore flicked the butt of the lit cigarette at Brayden. In the same instant, he lunged forward, bringing a short sword—a gladius—up from where he'd held it along his leg. Vittore darted forward, swung the sword in a tight arch, aiming for Brayden's head. The dark man skipped lightly out of reach.

"Honorable as ever," Brayden said.

"You're a beast, an animal. You should have died with the rest of your kind," Vittore hissed.

"You should have left with the rest of yours."

Another swing. Brayden slid under the blow, but the tip of the sword caught the neck of his sweater. It ripped, leaving one arm bare from shoulder to elbow. A thin stain of blood welled and trickled, marring the pale skin.

Deitra searched the cairn for a suitable chunk of slate to throw to distract Vittore. She heaved it at his head. It went wide, crashing into a crumbling headstone, pulverizing it.

Both men froze. Vittore's head whipped towards her.

"No!" he shouted, charging her like a maddened bull.

Brayden dashed across the graveyard to her side, enfolding her in his arms. Vittore slammed into them, knocking them to the ground.

"Uff!" Deitra grunted. She landed hard with Brayden on top of her. Groaning, he rolled off. She could see an ugly smear of blood along his naked side, the sweater nearly torn away now.

"What the hell?" she screamed, but Vittore attacked again, the sword whistling through the air toward Brayden's neck. Again, the dark man avoided the blow by fractions of an inch.

Deitra staggered to her feet. Brayden was up too, blood slicking his side from ribs to thigh. He stood between her and Vittore, but the blonde man refocused his attention on Brayden. His eyes flicked to the deep wound in Brayden's side and a cocky smile curved his lips.

"Far too long, Fey," Vittore growled. He circled Brayden, wolfish, his posture relaxed almost triumphant. "Tonight, your feast night, you join your ancestors."

"You never even tried to understand us, Romano, didja? You come to me tonight of all nights, with the mists around us. You're a brave fool, I give ya that," Brayden said. He waved at Deitra, motioning her back up the trail, back toward the distant twinkling lights of the inn. She ran a few steps, looked back.

Brayden stood, bare to the waist, head thrown back as if to embrace the night sky. Around him the mist surged like a living thing, roiling and wrapping him in its white tendrils. With his pale skin, he seemed to melt into it.

Vittore screamed, a wordless sound of rage and frustration. He plunged his sword into Brayden's unprotected chest, driving it in to the hilt.

Deitra wanted to scream, to vomit, to faint. Instead, she stood, rooted to the spot, only a few strides away from Brayden. The hot copper tang of blood was thick in the air.

Vittore let out a bark of laughter.

"Roma victor!" he shouted, raising his bloodied sword to the sky.

Deitra found her legs. Trembling she retraced her steps down the hillside.

Brayden was gone. An inky pool of blood marked where he'd stood.

Deitra glared at Vittore. He too stared at the empty spot. For a moment, the world held its breath. The wind died down and the mist settled. Frost tipped the lichen and moss, the curling ivy and thistles twinning around the grave markers. Westward, down the steep hill, the surf rolled. Above, the stars shone on, indifferent.

"How could you?" Deitra's voice was harsh. She looked around, wishing for a sword of her own.

"It was an abomination. A blight. It's their fault..." Vittore began.

"Our fault what?"

Brayden stood in the archway, grinning playfully. He

held a long, thin sword. It curved up slightly at the tip. Even in the faint moonlight, Deitra could see it was a beautiful piece, silvery and inscribed. It looked like something Jerrold might have displayed in his study.

Both men sprang forward. Deitra skipped back as their swords met and slid along, blades caressing like old lovers, parted, and met again. Most of Deitra's knowledge of swordplay had been gleaned from Robin Hood movies. She understood little of the finer detail.

Vittore attacked in short, powerful bursts. He advanced, turned, advanced again. Brayden gave ground before him, circled, danced, spun, his sword a blur. He seemed to rely on his agility to outmaneuver the Roman.

Brayden darted forward, twisted his blade past Vittore's guard. Vittore uttered a cry, his sword spinning away, clattering against the headstones. Brayden touched his sword to the other man's throat. The blade must have been fantastically sharp, as a line a blood welled instantly, falling to stain Vittore's jacket.

"Enough shite," Brayden said. "Yield. Leave our lands once and for all, Romano."

Vittore's face contorted in a snarl of rage and defeat. He sagged, his upraised hands falling to his lap. "I never thought it would come to this," he said.

"Off wicha," Brayden said. "We don't want your gods, your roads or your—"

His words were cut off as Vittore surged up, a small knife in his hand. He aimed for Brayden's neck, but the dark man dodged away, and the knife sunk into his shoulder, buried to the hilt.

Brayden swung his sword, so swift and sharp it barely paused as it sliced through Vittore's neck, severing his head from his body.

Deitra gasped and covered her mouth, watching as Vittore's body crumpled into a pile of dust and old bones.

Brayden held out a hand to her, but it wavered. His brow knit in a puzzled frown. He glanced at the wound in his chest. Dark veins spidered out from it, spreading across Brayden's pale chest.

"Iron," he said.

Brayden reached out to steady himself, missed the wall, and sat down hard. His sword clattered away. She could hear his breathing, quick and shallow.

"No!" cried Deitra. It wasn't fair. "But you won," she said as if she could argue with the corruption spreading from the wound. "What can I do? How can I help you?"

"Easy now, *a stòr*. Help is on the way," Brayden muttered, his voice low, strained. "We travel in packs."

Out of the mist strode Fáthach and Salix. Fáthach seemed to have grown about a foot or so, his skin a dark greyish color that blended into the rain-washed hills. Salix's hair blew around her as if caught by a wind no one else could feel. It had a strange, leafy quality and looked more deep forest green than dark brunette. Her skin was a soft, nut brown.

Deitra rose, unsure what to do. Around her, the mist

seemed to boil. She could see dark shapes moving through it, just beyond the graveyard.

"The Roman is gone?" Salix asked. Deitra nodded.

"The curse is broken, Prince." Fáthach's voice was a deep rumble, mingling with the crash of the surf below. There was another sound growing, far off, drawing closer through the mist. Pounding hoofs and beating wings.

Salix knelt at Brayden's side. Deitra did the same. The knife's corruption had spread to his jaw, black tendrils crawling up his cheeks.

Salix reached for the knife hilt but drew her hand back, hissing in pain. The hilt smoked, and Brayden groaned, biting his lip.

"Iron," Salix said, her voice the soft moan of wind through willow branches.

"Cursed Roman!" the giant growled. Great chalky tears rolled down his face. He lifted Brayden's silver sword, set the tip over Brayden's heart. "I'm so sorry, my lord."

"Wait." Deitra grabbed the giant's wrist. It felt like the rocks of the cairn. "Before, he healed. I can take the knife out. Would he be able to heal again?"

"We can only hope," Salix said. "Hurry, human. Don't make him suffer."

It was hard to get a good grip on the knife. It was deeply embedded, and the hilt slick with Brayden's blood. Every time she fumbled, Brayden jerked in pain. The giant held him down. Finally, Dietra managed to yank the knife free. She threw it as far as she could. Brayden sighed, his eyes fluttering closed.

"Brayden?" Deitra shook him. "Brayden. Brayden, wake up!"

"Peace," the willowy woman murmured, stroking Deitra's cheek. "He needs a moment only, to draw strength from the mist."

Deitra wiped tears from her eyes and looked around. The graveyard was surrounded by ghostly figures, some human-like, others animalistic, or strange combinations of both. All waited silently.

The gold eyes were still closed, but the barest hint of a grin tugged at the corner of Brayden's mouth. "He's awake!" Deitra cried.

"Shh," he whispered. He reached up and pulled her head down, brushed her lips with his. "Thank you." She kissed him fiercely. He tasted of spice and sunlight, of wind and rain and life.

"My prince," Salix said. "It is time to go home."

"A moment," Brayden said.

"It is nearly dawn," Fáthach said, a distant avalanche of sound. The eastern rim of the sky blushed a faint blue. The stars faded. Far, far away a bell tolled, calling the faithful to All Soul's mass.

"Please," Salix said. Around them the mist thinned, the shapes of ancient warriors and wild hunters vanishing with it. "Hurry."

Brayden searched Deitra's face, his gold eyes seeming

to touch her very core. "I have reason to stay," he said.

"Your mother sorrows at your absence. Your promise is kept. The land is free of the Roman. You must return home." Salix took a few steps and stopped, her whole body straining towards the waiting mist.

Brayden tore his eyes away from Deitra to glare at the woman. "Ever the dutiful one, Salix." He stood easily, no hint of injury. The black veins had vanished, leaving his skin smooth and perfect.

"We owe you our lord's life. If you ever need true aid, call for Fáthach," the giant said. He patted Deitra's shoulder hard enough to nearly knock her over. She clutched Brayden.

"I will come back, if I can," Brayden took her hand and pulled her close, touched his forehead to hers.

"That's not good enough," Deitra said. "I can't just go back now. I can't..." *Live without you.* It sounded so desperate. She wouldn't say it. What if he didn't feel the same?

"And I can't live without you. I knew the moment I saw you. There was something between us. Twin souls long separated." Brayden glanced around at the lightening sky, the evaporating mist. "I can't stay. I wish I could. I'll find you, *a stòr*."

He stepped away, following Fáthach and Salix into the mist. Her heart went with him. She drew a ragged breath.

"Wait!" She sprinted down the hill, into the mist. "I'm going with you."

Brayden turned. "And give up your mortal life?" He was starting to fade with the mist, only his dark hair, gold eyes, and impish smile stood out plainly.

"And gain you," Deitra said.

Brayden held out a hand, and she took it. As he drew her into the shinning mist, she looked back. They rose through the air, leaving behind the cool, windswept hills, the ancient stone walls, the warm hearths, and human world.

"It's funny," Deitra said, nestling her head against Brayden's shoulder as he spread his great dark wings. "I think I may just miss England after all."

Maiden Voyage of the Fearless

Claudine Griggs

"Bite down hard," said the nurse.

Antoinette felt almost insulted. "I've done this before," she said, neither worried nor happy about the procedure. Despite her severe anxiety disorder, which was why he was here, the treatments were routine, and Antoinette liked routine.

The nurse spread conductive gel on Antoinette's temples. The doctor positioned the electrode paddles. "Ready," he said, more out of habit than necessity, and stepped on the foot pedal to administer electroshock therapy to his patient.

Because the treatments were moderately helpful, Antoinette Rodriguez and her parents requested they be administered twice per year in addition to the usual medications for stress and depression. At age 34, Antoinette still lived with her parents, typically left her bedroom only for specially prepared meals, and almost never ventured outside the Rodriguez residence except to the hospital for biannual "electroconvulsive therapy."

ECT was rarely used because many medical practitioners considered it barbaric. The procedure certainly looked barbaric, with its purposefully induced seizures caused by shooting electricity into the brain while restraining the patient on a table. The nurses, especially young women new to the profession, typically found it more distasteful than the doctors, but everyone who had worked with Antoinette during her two decades of psychiatric care agreed. She needed these treatments.

Pharmaceuticals, hypnosis, and counseling could do only so much, and even with enhanced anxiety medications, Antoinette was a curious case: acute agoraphobia compounded by depression, obsessive compulsive disorder, and other issues that could not be precisely labeled. Off the record, people said, "The woman's terrified of everything." Antoinette even worried about the day when her loving parents might abandon her, or die, or murder her and stuff the body into an industrial meat grinder to dispose of the evidence.

Antoinette understood that there were no rational bases for most of her fears, but by age 14 she had begun to have severe social difficulties. Too many people on campus. Too many at the shopping mall. Too many strangers. In fifth-period history class at Brookline High, Massachusetts, she started answering questions that had not been asked, and the teacher informed her parents. By age 15, with so many people "thinking bad thoughts," with so much danger everywhere, Antoinette refused to leave her bedroom.

To the relief of the school authorities, the doctor transferred her to a psychiatric hospital in Belmont, where she screamed hysterically about people trying to kill her and then cowered in a corner whenever left alone. Too many lab coats. Too much stimulation. Too much terror.

After four months of observation, medications, and electroconvulsive therapy, a psychiatric panel agreed that Antoinette Rodriguez was permanently disabled by mental illness. She would probably never be able to work, buy groceries, establish social relationships, or care for herself. She even had difficulty sleeping because dreams frightened her (insomnia added to the neurological troubles), and she resisted exercise because the strain might induce a heart attack. Antoinette wondered whether even her shadow, which occasionally tried to console her, might turn malicious. A strong anti-anxiety and anti-depressant compound helped, but despite knowledgeable and compassionate doctors, Antoinette pleaded for the security of her own room.

"Like chicken soup," said Dr. William Crawford to her parents, "homecare couldn't hurt. And it might even help as we try different therapies."

So, Antoinette returned to her familiar bedroom with a prescription, regular nursing visits, and biannual electroshock therapy. ECT worked better than anything else at temporarily calming the patient—enough, at least, so that Antoinette could function with the in-house supervision of her parents. The insurance company supported the plan as well because it cost significantly less than inpatient hospital care.

Mr. and Mrs. Rodriguez worried what might happen to Antoinette should one or both of them die. They languished over grandchildren that would never be. They prayed that Antoinette would get better but, especially, that she would not get worse. And the deeply religious Rodriguezes accepted God's purpose, whatever it may be, in the special care required of their daughter.

* * *

Thus, from age 15, Antoinette lived in her small bedroom with adjoining bath for the better part of 18 years, cleaning and sanitizing her living space every Wednesday and Saturday at 2:00 p.m. She had a desk, computer, and online access that included free library accounts and streaming via Netflix, Amazon, and HBO. There was no phone because Antoinette feared direct calls; thus, all communications from the doctors or would-be friends passed through Mr. and Mrs. Rodriguez, who talked through the door or passed notes under it. Antoinette generally accepted instructions from her mother or father as long as the messages were handwritten with a designated code number penned at the bottom. The code changed weekly. Her bedroom door remained locked at all times, though Mr. and Mrs.

Rodriguez had a key, and Antoinette emerged for meals when summoned by the signal knock—dot, dot, dash, dash, dot, dot—followed by the words "Edgar's raven is not flitting." Antoinette trusted her parents as long as the codes and signals matched. Someone could impersonate them, and impersonators would be bad.

Mr. and Mrs. Rodriguez consented to all of Antoinette's requests. They had once considered corporeal punishment to pressure their daughter's socialization, which was strongly recommended by a family friend from Tennessee, but the Rodriguezes trusted in the therapeutic value of love. Besides, the medications and electroconvulsive treatments seemed violent enough. What could coercion accomplish for Antoinette? And, more to the point, Mr. and Mrs. Rodriguez absolutely cherished their daughter, and they would wait patiently for a medical miracle to come along—and they believed it would come.

God was good. God was merciful.

* * *

The miracle came. Pharmaceutical researchers developed what was informally called "courage in a bottle," and the first-stage animal trials had remarkably decreased anxiety in some of the most timid creatures imaginable. A cat that cowered under the sofa when any stranger arrived suddenly became a lap kitty for all visitors. A subordinate capuchin monkey turned calm, grew back its full body hair, and, when threatened, seemed almost anxious to fight other capuchins; however, the smaller, medicated, monkey did not become aggressive unless provoked. A mixed-breed shelter dog that had never lifted its tail from between its legs could suddenly trust humans, wag its whole body from tip to stern, tug on its leash to explore new territories, and appear ecstatic about everything it met. The previously abandoned animal was adopted by a research technician who noted that the Ferralyxis-infused pooch could sometimes be too happy to control.

* * *

Doctors and researchers quickly targeted Antoinette Rodriguez as a prime candidate for the human trials of Ferralyxis. She had spent 18 years in self-exile, essentially leaving home only for electroconvulsive therapy. Antoinette's parents were eager to test the medication on their daughter, hoping it might be the long-solicited miracle from heaven. Antoinette, however, resisted all persuasive efforts, for she long ago surrendered to the anxieties that were much stronger than she could ever be. She had grown comfortable in her protected life with a computer window to the external world.

"Happiness is a locked room," thought Antoinette. But while she sought security now and forever, her parents worried about a dark future where trees fell in the forest and made no sound because their daughter would never even attempt to hear them. After praying on the matter, Mr. and Mrs. Rodriguez signed consent forms to begin

Antoinette's treatment with Ferralyxis.

Dr. Crawford (Antoinette's psychiatrist) and Dr. Kovack (a pharmaceutical executive) visited Antoinette at home for the first therapeutic injection, which could not be administered because the patient barricaded her bedroom door when she heard their car pull into the driveway. This was not completely unexpected. Antoinette defended herself thusly against all intruders. Even Dr. Crawford, whom she trusted as much as she could anyone beyond her parents, failed to persuade her out of the bedroom for treatment. Irrational fear is its own defense, and since age 15, Antoinette's had been nearly insurmountable.

"It's all right, Antoinette," said Dr. Crawford through the door. "We won't force our way. I'll come back alone and talk with you another time."

The doctors both knew that Antoinette's regular ECT was set for 11:00 a.m. the following Thursday. They would simply administer the Ferralyxis then.

Antoinette always kept those appointments. She was afraid not to.

* * *

Antoinette's 32nd electroconvulsive therapy session proceeded much like all the others she had endured, almost enjoyed. They provided a degree of relaxation that could be counted on. Not a cure, but a change of pace, a different drummer. Combined with the sedative after Antoinette regained consciousness, ECT was similar to what other folks might feel when visiting a bar for whiskey and companionship. Something to do. Something to buzz the brain and body. But today, along with Antoinette's regular treatment, she unknowingly received a first dose of Ferralyxis before returning to the warm embrace of her bedroom.

Her parents had hope. Antoinette did not possess the knowledge to have hope.

* * *

The doctors provided Mr. and Mrs. Rodriguez with liquid Ferralyxis and instructed them to add five drops to Antoinette's lunchtime Kool-Aid, her favorite beverage, though she heated it to 182 degrees in a large coffee mug to destroy any lurking bacteria. At dinner, she preferred cherry flavored sparkling water straight from the bottle after washing the neck with disinfectant and then rinsing with distilled water, a ritual that had continued for 18 years. Antoinette's food was likewise scrutinized, and Mrs. Rodriguez had long ago learned to prepare nutritious meals that were satisfactory to her daughter, though Mrs. Rodriguez waited for a day when the meticulous routines might change.

That time, hopefully, had come. Medical professionals advised Mr. and Mrs. Rodriguez that Ferralyxis would probably require weeks or months to accumulate in Antoinette's brain with noticeable effects, but since she was the first human patient, precise effects could be neither predicted nor guaranteed. The initial dosage was minimal, based on animal tests, and would be gradually increased according to Antoinette's progress. The possibility remained that Ferralyxis would not benefit humans, so expectations should be curtailed until outcomes were confirmed and calibrated. Medical science worked this way.

Antoinette's parents did not care to think about failure. Their daughter presently clung to the bottom rung of Jacob's ladder.

"Nothing to lose," they agreed. "Everything to gain."

The first Ferralyxis Kool-Aid was repeated day by day, but for Mr. and Mrs. Rodriguez, that initial dose marked the beginning toward a new world. Similar optimism resided in the doctors and nurses, parents and friends, and pharmaceutical investors—everyone but Antoinette, who remained strategically unaware of the miracle drug pulsing through her body.

* * *

Antoinette responded quickly to treatment and within three weeks took her lunch beverage over ice. She likewise began to spend a few afternoons in the living room, watching TV and talking with her mother about places and things she had read about online. The fifth week, Antoinette greeted her father upon his return from work and hugged him, something she had not done since age 12—and this hug proved noticeably more convincing.

Mr. Rodriguez treasured the surprise embrace of his daughter but asked, "Aren't you afraid of germs?"

immediately wishing he hadn't.

Antoinette giggled and squeezed him even tighter. "You're worth the risk, Papi."

After seven weeks, Antoinette visited a local park with both parents, climbed on a swing, and laughed out loud as she re-learned how to make it go. Later, they all went to a burger restaurant for lunch. Antoinette ordered her sandwich well-done, which still seemed sensible, but used ketchup from the table on her fries. She also tasted beer for the first time in her life. Through years of reading she could describe hundreds of varieties, how they were brewed, differences in color and clarity and effervescence, but having missed the actual experience of taste, she could not know the bubbled flavor of 34-degree Budweiser from a frosted mug.

Antoinette grimaced on the first sip and pushed the pint toward her father. "I think this will be an acquired taste!"

She then ventured sparkling water with a squeeze of fresh lime. "Now that's good!" she said after downing half the bottle without sterilizing the neck. Tears began to flow as she added, "But the best part is where I am…out in the world with my parents…who always stood by me." She paused and kissed her father and mother on each cheek. "How could you love such a pathetic daughter all those years?"

Antoinette did not expect an answer, and her mother began to cry too.

"How could we not?" said Mrs. Rodriguez.

Antoinette knew a lot about love and hardship and sacrifice. She'd read millions of words on many subjects. But like the taste of alcohol, there was no way to measure emotional flavors without relevant experience. How could she possibly grasp her parents' devotion? To Antoinette, heartfelt family bonds seemed as illogical as they were beautiful.

* * *

A year later, Antoinette could not be contained. After 19 years of seclusion, she became a runner, backpacker, and climber. Her goals included visiting every U.S. National Park that she'd read about from her bedroom computer. After that, she'd explore South America, Europe, Asia, Australia, Africa, and the moon if it ever opened to tourism. Her ambitions became imperatives—a new kind of anxiety—because she'd missed almost half a lifetime of mental incapacitation. "Fear," she decided, "is a vampire on the human spirit." Antoinette would abide no more of that, and she would account for every drop of embezzled lifeblood.

Fortunately, Mr. and Mrs. Rodriguez could afford Antoinette's adventures and willingly provided leeway in their daughter's extraordinary rehabilitative passions. However, they became moderately concerned 36 weeks into treatment when Antoinette, during a gymnasium workout, confronted a "bully" (Antoinette's term) who proved reluctant to share the free weights with women.

"It seems," said the 145-pound Antoinette to the man, "that you have a certain possessiveness about our workout space." She had limited social skills and sounded more hostile than intended.

"What's that to you?" asked the 210-pound, heavily muscled, 6-foot-2 Adonis wannabe.

Antoinette didn't get angry immediately. This seemed like a straightforward question. "Well," she responded, "everyone pays for membership and should qualify for equal access and all that."

"How about I give you equal access to mops and buckets to clean the bathrooms, Brown Sugar. Why don't you get at it?"

Even Antoinette recognized this slander to women and Hispanics. Still, she spoke calmly. "Instead, how about I shove the handle end of a mop up your ass. Or maybe the bucket upside your head."

The man slapped Antoinette hard across the jaw. Her face felt like it exploded, but she stood straight and smiled, a small trickle of blood leaking from the side of her lip.

"Thank you," she began with a slow, calculated pace. "No one has hit ever me. It's much more educational than reading about misogynistic violence on my computer."

The man pondered her response, suspected that Antoinette might be mentally deficient, and made a half-witted apology. "Maybe that'll learn you some manners, honey. I don't like hitting a woman even when she deserves it."

Antoinette glanced downward and turned sideways to relax the man's guard. Then she tore into his 210-pound frame without restraint. She knew every point of anatomy and slammed the side of her palm hard against his larynx. As he began to choke and reflexively clutched his throat with both hands, she squared her body and lifted a knee into his groin with a bountiful squish. Adonis went down and stayed down.

Paramedics barely saved the man's life with an on-site tracheotomy. Patrons defended Antoinette's actions as self-defense—no one much liked Adonis man anyway—but her gym membership was revoked. She didn't care. There were many fitness centers, and the righteous warmth from crushing an aggressor agreed with her.

Dr. Crawford reduced Antoinette's Ferralyxis prescription, which she now took with informed consent, in response to the incident. "Such is the nature of human trials," he told Mr. and Mrs. Rodriguez. "No one yet knows a therapeutic level from an overdose." He did not say that surplus courage with deficit fear could be dangerous. Besides, as Antoinette grew stronger and happier month by month, the medication seemed a modern miracle, and she commandeered each daily measure with terrible resolve.

* * *

Antoinette began to march up Yosemite Falls trail at 6:05 a.m. sharp. Her goals included a conditioning climb to the upper falls, allowing nineteen minutes for rest breaks and snacks. Then she would hike to the edge of El Capitan and ultimately retrace her steps to the valley floor before dark. Early October would offer gentle weather and only a small trickle from Yosemite Creek. And as luck would have it, the day's forecast was 72 degrees with scattered white clouds and a soft breeze. Perfect.

As usual, Antoinette hiked alone with a well-equipped daypack that included the ten essentials in case of emergency. Solitary ventures suited her best. She could ascend and descend without delays inflicted by an out-of-shape or under-motivated partner. Further, the Yosemite trails were well-traveled, and if needed, assistance would be available, and cellphone service at the summit registered three bars. Antoinette worried more about her training and conditioning than injury.

She loved the national parks, especially Yosemite and Zion. Her rock climbing skills were improving, and today's trail trek preceded a planned assault on El Capitan's face in five months. This would require more technical practice and a likely partner, but the problem for Antoinette remained that most climbers were cowards who couldn't meet her rigid standards. The goal was everything. And she had already missed out on too much life to hold back on account of nervous fools.

Still, Antoinette watched for telltale signs of human courage and determination. If she had been cured with Ferralyxis, others would inevitably follow. Then she might find a worthy partner. In the meantime, she must tolerate weakling peasants.

Antoinette's quadriceps already burned from exertion-induced lactate. She increased the pace.

* * *

Antoinette Rodriguez conquered the trail in seven hours and forty-eight minutes. Not as fast as she would have liked, but respectable.

She stood at the rim of El Capitan, her boots four inches from the edge, and looked across Yosemite Valley. A stiff breeze raced up the cliff and brought water to her eyes. She wondered how she had ever lived in a tiny bedroom, in her tiny mind, afraid of places and feelings such as these.

Antoinette checked her Marathon watch and set the chronometer. She would allow twenty-one minutes to enjoy the view, snack on a protein-and-carb trail mix, rehydrate, and begin retracing her route to the valley floor. That was the plan, anyway. But as she marveled at Yosemite with Ferralyxis-enhanced emotion, a small earthquake rattled the ground along a minor slip-strike fault, as often happens in California. This was not a temblor that would make news beyond professional geologists—a 2.8 on the Richter scale, centered 3 miles north of El Capitan, and barely noticeable. But Antoinette noticed. A soft roll and a rumble.

Standing several feet away stood a rugged, handsome looking man with his German shepherd on a sturdy leather leash. The dog apparently also heard the temblor and growled toward nothing in particular. Antoinette disliked the throaty sound, though a dog might be forgiven for primitive instincts and lack of human intelligence, but she slipped the backpack from her shoulders and discretely removed a combat-ready Buck Knife. She opened the freshly honed blade and firmed her stance. Even as she consciously tried to calm her adrenaline response, she figured it couldn't hurt to be prepared.

Antoinette held silent for several seconds but finally said to the young man, "I'm sorry, but don't like threats, even from an animal. They make me edgy."

"Oh," said the kind-hearted man, "please forgive us. My dog's name is Questor, and we love hiking together. I'm sure the growl wasn't at you. He's loved everybody since he was a pup. Guess he's a little edgy, too." Trying to assure her further he added, "I'm actually surprised by this behavior. But don't worry. I've a firm grip on the leash."

However, as often happens after movement along a fault, there soon followed a mild aftershock just as Antoinette tried to calm herself in measure of the man's response. The time, the dog flinched and barked at the sky.

Antoinette vaulted toward Questor, grabbed his collar, and both went over the side of El Capitan. The young man followed because he tried to save his dog by holding onto the leather strap. He was strong, but not strong enough for the combined weight of a German shepherd and muscular woman propelled into thin air.

Antoinette had intended to jam her blade into Questor's ribs, but she immediately released the animal's collar as they plummeted.

This is glorious, she thought. *To free fall through space. To live without fear. To embrace every challenge.* A spectacular moment in a spectacular life.

The valley floor approached very fast. The air burned Antoinette's skin and tore at her deep brown eyes, which remained strong and beautiful and unblinking. Questor's threat was now completely forgotten as a new enemy approached—just seconds away—an enemy that could not be defeated but could still be opposed.

Antoinette flashed a smile as she had done with the gymnasium Adonis. Her last bit of glory in a single instant of battle against the Earth. She prepared for a knife thrust into the ground. She would show no mercy.

* * *

The Boston Globe reported, "Antoinette Rodriguez of Brookline, Massachusetts, Jonathan Krieger of Thousand Oaks, California, and his beloved dog Questor slipped to their deaths yesterday from Yosemite's El Capitan.

"Sadly, according to witnesses, the dog became agitated after a small earthquake and may have pulled against his leash, causing Krieger to lose balance. It is believed that Antoinette Rodriguez tried to grab Questor in an attempt to prevent their fall. But, unfortunately, all three tumbled over the edge.

"Doctors stated that Rodriguez had once suffered from extreme anxiety disorder, but treatment with a miraculous new drug enabled her to begin life as a vibrant and adventurous young woman. The clinical trials with Ferralyxis exceeded all expectations, and her recovery had been widely documented in leading medical journals. Unfortunately, as this new Wonder Woman stood on top of El Capitan, celebrating a vigorous morning hike, she lost her life trying to save others. This was a great tragedy not only for Rodriguez, Krieger, Questor, and their families, but for medical research as well. Still, doctors want to assure people suffering from acute anxiety that testing of Ferralyxis will continue, and the miracle drug should soon be FDA approved for general psychiatric prescriptions.

"According to Dr. William Crawford, her treating physician, 'Antoinette Rodriguez did not live or die in vain, because many others will someday replicate her triumph over mental illness.'"

The Becoming

Taylor Buccello

Humans don't remember every second of the day. It's not something the consciousness can handle. Now, The Chosen, they're different. The Becoming gives them one day to remember everything, yet wish they'd experienced nothing.

On whatever day your god chooses, you wake to the zero hour bells. Because of the aching deep in your joints and muscles, you give up on trying to fall back to sleep. By the third hour, you're completely awake.

No matter how much you stretch or walk or run, no matter how many hot baths or concoctions you take, the aches persist, getting worse until the mere thought of breathing makes your chest hurt.

Aches and pains, now those can be hidden, can be written off as being tired or slipping into some sickness. Seizures can't. They're a statement. Gods love attention, they crave it. The shrines, the thunderstorms, the sacrifices—they thrive off it. They'd die without it.

The eighth hour: school or work for the lucky ones and the opening of the market for the rest. The eighth hour is when you can no longer deny you have been Chosen.

The shaking begins with gentle tremors, like you're stuck in one of the cold Districts without a cloak or a shawl. Then, your legs and arms and entire being begin to shake so badly the world blurs—colors bleeding together and faces smearing across your vision.

By the ninth hour, your muscles start to calm, but not because of whatever the doctor or apothecary has forced down your throat or into your blood. Medicine doesn't do anything to ease The Becoming. Priests can do nothing. Prayers and sacrifices are worthless. Mortal attempts to relieve suffering are no match against the plans of the gods.

The ninth hour is bliss compared to what came before. Compared to what is coming.

The pain recedes—still there, but less. A pot near boiling with bubbles trapped on the bottom of the bowl, not yet shaking the water or smothering the air above with steam. Not yet choking the water with heat, but slowly building the temperature.

Slowly—oh so slowly building the agony. Building until your heart is pounding and frantic, your breathing heavy and strained. Until you're soaked in a cold sweat and the sheets of the clinic bed are stuck to your skin and your hair is matted across your head. And you're cold.

You're so cold the shaking comes back. Not caused by the gods, not this time, but by your own body fighting against the frost creeping up your fingers and toes.

At the eleventh hour, a wheel spoke drives itself into your head. Not literally. It only feels literal, as though your fingers would come back sticky with blood if you were to touch a hand to your head.

Every heartbeat, every breath, every footfall or spoken word—it all worms into your mind and rattles around. It's a game of Lines, except, instead of shaking a dozen marbles in your hands, you're shaking shards of glass in your head.

The twelfth hour is the worst.

When the bells of the twelfth hour near, you're afraid. You're so utterly fearful that the sound of bronze rod striking bronze bell will finally crack your skull open. The anxious tension in your chest becomes so tight you begin to believe your heart will stop under the pressure, blood stilling in your veins as you wait for the end. Stilling, sitting, rotting.

When the bells finally ring, the headache vanishes and takes your vision with it.

Blind, you can't see the panic of those around you when they watch your eyes drain of all normal color. Every part fills with a red so deep that, before we knew about The Becoming, the doctors thought The Chosen were bleeding in their minds and had no hope left. Granted, at this hour, The Chosen have forsaken any hope of survival and traded it for the hope of death and the peace it ought to bring. Life in The Underworld *must* be better than The Becoming. *Anything* must be better.

Those who fail to meet the standards of the gods, their eyes don't turn back. The Cursed Ones, they're called. Their sight never returns, their voices soon following. Their sanity, too, in some cases. Living in utter darkness with no ability to express themselves, it's hard for them to make it back to reality.

With sight cut out of your world, the rest of reality begins to slip away to join it buried in the back of your mind. Buried underneath the visions, underneath the voices and the delusions.

It's hard to know when the hallucinations begin. The Chosen are too far from the rest of the world to ask about a sundial or candle to tell how much time has passed. The screaming usually begins near the thirteenth hour.

The visions are different for each person. They're for understanding, I've been told. Understanding the life of the god that chose you—because there can't be anything worse than a Chosen who doesn't value the power of their god.

Minan's Chosen thrashed in his bed for hours as the goddess of war showed him battle after battle after battle. The Chosen for Sofiia, goddess of beauty and education, surfaced from The Becoming in tears over the dangers of ignorance. The god of love and dreams, Lazari, drowned his Chosen in stories of great and terrible romances, of dreams that flourish and dreams that collapse and take their dreamers down with.

I was shown thousands of deaths and grieving families and rewards and punishments. No living human knows what The Underworld is like, yet. I was given a tour by the goddess of death, afterlife herself.

None of the visions are pleasant. The lives and duties of the gods are never pleasant, not to humans who don't have the same capacities for apathy and strength. For weeks, the visions linger, piecing themselves into your life. When you're living lives thousands of years longer than your own, only so much can fit into half a day. The rest have to come in the form of phantom voices and all-consuming flashbacks.

It all feels so real—the feelings are so real. The *sensations* are so lifelike you begin to feel as though you've been completely removed from your real life. You begin to convince yourself your real life was the dream, the hallucination, and this one, this dark and cold and lonely life is what is yours. It takes a lot to hold on to yourself during those hours.

The fever hits during the twentieth hour. If The Chosen weren't protected by the gods, their minds would melt from the heat.

The bleeding begins at the twenty-third hour and doesn't stop until the day's candles have nearly melted down to nothing. The best move on the part of doctors is to put The Chosen in the bath when the fever hits and not to take them out until the day is over. Otherwise, the blood leaking from their mouths and noses and eyes and ears will soak through their bed sheets and into the mattress.

The Chosen wake from their nightmare when the candles are nothing more than a thin film, translucent over the metal base. They wake for long enough to throw up the contents of their stomach, drink a cup of water, and smile to their mother, if they're fortunate enough to still have her around.

Then, when the zero hour bells chime, they collapse, falling into a sleep that lasts the next three days. When they wake, everything from that day has disappeared. The only sign any of it happened comes from the memories of those around them and The Mark.

Like the visions, The Mark is different for each person. For some, it's small, nothing more than a flower the size of a fingernail on their collarbone. For others, they wake up with intricate wings stained into their back and shoulders. With the outline of a lily flower drenched in red and its black leaves framing my right eye, I have no chance of forgetting or pretending not to be Chosen.

It's a damned infestation, if you ask me. The gods check to see if you're a worthy host, one capable of keeping them alive, then take over and start cleaning out their new home. It's an epidemic of gods moving in. I see at least three a week being brought into Dr. Nal's shop. Gods that haven't been seen in years are showing up and claiming their—

"I'm hungry."

I sigh, shaking my head to draw back my focus. Having a voice in your mind that isn't yours could be quite distracting.

"You're hungry, too. I know you are."

I have yet to find a way to drown out Runa's voice. Something about her being a goddess made it so nothing could outshine her when she didn't want it to.

"Come on, Vae. Let's take a break and go get some of that...whatever you call it, the sweet thing, from the market."

I pick up the washing bucket and set it on the floor. Grabbing a rag, I start drying off the surgical tools on the counter.

"Vaera. Vaera. Vae. Vae. Vae. Come on. Vae."

I slam down the scalpel in my hands. "I can't take a break whenever you want pastries! That's not how it works here!"

The head nurse, Josef, raises an eyebrow from his desk on the other side of the room.

"Sorry," I say, ducking my head and going back to drying the tools I had just washed.

"People are staring. They think you're crazed," Runa says. *"They won't let you work if you're insane. Come on, let's go get pahsterees."*

I squeeze my eyes shut, taking a breath. Throwing the tools into their bin, I set it back in the cabinet and rest my forehead on the cool wood of the door.

For The Chosen, The Becoming may only last a day, but the gods, they never go away.

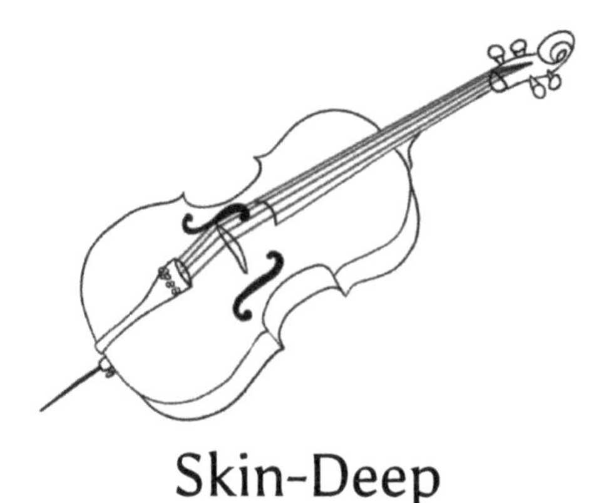

Skin-Deep

Julia Figliotti

Her name had been Shelly for as long as she could remember. But then again, she had been his for as long as she could remember. Her previous life was not important, nor was the name she used to go by.

She was Shelly, and she was his. That was all she needed to know. That was all she had ever known.

When he first came to own her, he took her to a tattoo parlor and told her to agree to whatever it was that he said. She only nodded; following orders was not new to her. Pain was not new to her. He spoke with the tattoo artist—a friend of his, she guessed, judging by the lack of questions that the man seemed to have concerning the art and its canvas—and beckoned her over. The man asked her if she knew what the tattoo process was and if she was ready to begin. Again, Shelly only nodded. Pain was not new to her.

The man who owned her watched as she calmly

removed her shirt and bra and laid herself face down on the artist's table. Her russet hair swirled around her face, resting on the pillow that her head now claimed. The whir of the needle started, loud and low and constant, and she took a deep breath and closed her mind to it. But for the first time, she was brought sharply back to reality by a piercing, dragging pain, so acute yet so overwhelming, on the right side of her lower spine. She was shocked at the pain she felt. This pain was new to her.

For the next few hours—or was it only minutes? or was it days?—Shelly gritted her teeth against the ache that traveled slowly, methodically, up her back with the artist's needle. Long, straight lines were being etched into the skin that covered her spine, making her want to cry out in pain, though she knew that would not end well for her. She did not yet know the man who owned her, but from what she had seen of him so far, she knew that he was not a man to cross, and he was not a man who forgave.

When the needle reached the back of her neck, Shelly had to bite her tongue to keep herself quiet. She tasted the preface to blood in her mouth, and her saliva turned hot and sour. Pain blossomed from the trails that the artist's tool left in her skin, and she took the time to wonder how long it would take for her back to heal. She didn't even want to know what it looked like, and as long as she never turned her back to a mirror, she wouldn't have to. She tried not to concentrate on the curves and lines being torn into her unblemished skin. Instead, she concentrated on her new name. Shelly.

It appeared in writing in her mind, and she hated it. It looked stupid to her and sounded childish. What kind of man was this, anyway, to own her and mark her and call her by a name that belongs to a young girl? Shelly. Her mind was brought sharply back to the pain in her body, the whir in her ear, the taste in her mouth. Shelly.

Finally, blessedly, the whirring stopped. The artist put down his tools and rubbed a joltingly cold gel on the newly stained skin of her back. She winced with a passionate mix of joy and pain—joy from the reprieve of the artist's needle, which had dug so mercilessly into her skin, and from the healing qualities that she could feel as the aloe seeped into her pores. She felt pain from the harsh mixture of her open wounds and the shock of the cold ointment against her feverish skin.

Gently, the artist asked her to stand up slowly, telling her that he would show her to the mirror so she could admire the work of art that her blank canvas had become. She barely heard the pride in his voice that came from creating a masterpiece. With pleading eyes, she looked at the man who had brought her here. He stared blankly back at her, and she truly saw him for the first time.

He was tall, taller than her own five-foot-ten by at least four inches. His dark mustache was trimmed hastily around the top of his small mouth and down the sides, meeting up in a goatee with a strip of facial hair that began below the center of his lower lip and connected in a beard at the chin. His hair was raven black and down to his chest, thin but beautiful, with a streak of blonde that highlighted either side of his pale face. His eyes were a deep brown, chilling and exciting all at once, lower lids lined with a dark smudge. His nose was straight, a complement to his pronounced cheekbones and thick eyebrows.

He wore a fitted black suit jacket that covered a tight black shirt. A thick silver chain graced his collarbone and the base of his neck, shown off by a slight dip in his shirt. His leather fingerless gloves were worn with use, the fingers protruding from them long and clean. The man's long legs were clad in tight leather pants which boasted silver chains from pocket to pocket. His boots were as black as the rest of him, military style and untied. Shelly swallowed hard as he blinked once, seeming to come out of whatever trance he had been in.

"Get dressed," he told her, his low voice reeking of an unfamiliar accent that sent chills down her newly inked spine. "We don't have time for this." He turned to the artist, handed him some money—quite a lot of it, from what she could see—and turned back to Shelly, who had forsaken her bra and tight blouse in favor of a loose T-shirt the artist had given her. "We're leaving."

She followed him out of the small tattoo parlor, reading the instructions the artist had handed her on her way out. *Do not pick at the tattoo. Do not scratch or rub the tattoo. Pat the tattoo dry after bathing. Apply ointment daily for seven days.* Her bewildered mind struggled to process all of this while simultaneously wondering how on earth she would be able to reach the middle of her back in order to apply the ointment. This was all so new to her.

For the next week, he hardly spoke to her. She had assumed that he would use her in ways that she had been used before: cleaning, cooking, grooming, a quick fuck every now and then. But he asked nothing of her, except to come to his bedroom every morning when she woke so he could apply the ointment to her back. He did it with care, his long fingers sweeping wetly up and down her spine, caressing the raised, blackened skin that scarred her back. She got chills every time he touched her, but she knew she could not show it. A man was a dangerous thing, especially when she didn't know what it was that he wanted from her. When she left him every morning, his eyes were alive, shining with a hidden pleasure. When she saw him under any other circumstances, they were far off and empty. She got chills then, too.

For those first seven days, it took all of her willpower not to drag her nails across whatever skin on her back her long arms would let her reach, not to slam her back against the nearest wall corner and drag her body back and forth. But she had been warned about what could happen to her new art if she did that, and she didn't know what kind of reaction that would elicit from the man. And that was something she didn't want to find out.

The man had given her a room of her own in his house. It was not a dingy chamber in any way, but an actual bedroom. She had a spacious four-poster bed with canopy drapes and a firm mattress, a closet for her few clothes and belongings, an armchair and a loveseat, and a picture window that framed a beautiful little lake and a weeping willow tree. Across from the window was a floor-length mirror that beckoned to her daily, calling at her, begging her to see how the man had marked her as his own. Instead, she would look at her face, her hair, her body, noting that her brunette hair was still full of color, her hazel eyes were still bright with life, her cheeks were still pink, her lips full, her figure a small hourglass. These were the things that kept her sane. These were the things that kept her alive.

She went to him on the eighth morning, expecting to feel the chill of the ointment and the burning of his eyes on her back. But when she walked into the room, he didn't motion for her to turn around. He didn't tell her to remove her shirt. He only stared at her with his dull brown eyes, almost unseeingly. Shelly looked back at him, growing increasingly nervous at his lack of participation, debating whether or not to retreat from his darkened bedroom. She had just decided that her presence was not welcome when he spoke to her.

"Does it still itch at all?" He hadn't spoken so many words in her presence since the tattoo parlor. Shelly shook her head. "Does it hurt?" She shook her head again.

"Good." His eyes began to heat up, though her tattoo was shrouded entirely. She never thought she would see that fire begin to kindle; she had only ever seen it at full strength. His dull, dead look turned slowly into a tight interest, though his facial expression remained the same. Shelly had a moment to marvel at the power that the man's eyes held before he stood up abruptly, almost tricking her into a startled jump backwards. He began to walk towards her, slowly, staring at every part of her that he could see

"Do you know why I chose you?" Shelly's eyes widened; no one had ever asked her that question before. No one had ever spoken to her so softly, yet so dangerously. But then, she reminded herself, she had never belonged to anyone else. She stood rooted to the ground in dumb silence. "Do you know why I had to have you?" She blinked and shook her head. She didn't trust herself to speak at a time like this. Even the air around them seemed fragile, as though one wrong word would shatter it and send shards of ambiance into their skulls.

"It's your shape," the man said, taking another fluid step in Shelly's confused direction. "Your shape…and your hair. Your hair is like mahogany." His voice was shaking slightly with anticipation, making his thick accent almost unreadable. He held out a quivering hand towards her as he came within reach of her body. She had prepared for this. Pain was not new to her.

But he did not hurt her. He seemed afraid to even touch

her. When he finally closed the distance between them, he lowered his hand to his front pocket and extracted a thin brown ribbon that reminded Shelly of her own hair color. His eyes were on hers now, and she did not look away.

"Turn around, please," the man said, his now-even voice carefully controlled. She did as she was told, her instincts screaming at her not to turn her back on a man like this, but her practiced mind ignoring the warning. She felt expert hands run through her hair, twisting it into a low bun and securing it with the ribbon. The man turned her around so she was facing him and began to remove her shirt. She did nothing to dissuade him, nor did she assist him; this was the kind of man who did things his own way, the kind of man who would tell her when he wanted her to act. Deft fingers blindly unclasped her bra, the leather of his gloves scratching against her scarred back as her mind wandered just far enough that she could still hear his orders and read his eyes.

As Shelly was being undressed, her wandering mind focused on a tall wooden chair in the center of the man's bedroom. It was ancient and scuffed, a deep oaken color, carved with precision and care. The chair had no arms, no comfortable qualities that the eye could see. Its back was tall and straight and menacing. He led her to it slowly, his eyes still glowing with their secret flame.

Along the way, he removed his own shirt, revealing tattoos that covered his arms and shoulders and much of his slim chest. His fingerless gloves remained on his hands. He sat in the chair with his back rigid, his right arm worming behind the seat as though it were searching for something. When he brought it back to the front of his body, the man's hand grasped a long, thin strip of wood that boasted what seemed to be taut, fine white fibers. Horse hair, Shelly realized. She pushed the thought easily away. The man's legs were spread now, and he stared at her intensely, the fire in his eyes hotter now than she'd ever seen it.

"Kneel."

She slid easily onto practiced knees, the transition natural, the position comfortable. She knew what would come next—what else could it be? This man had just taken a little bit longer to get there than the others.

The man extracted another long, mahogany ribbon from his pocket and took both of her wrists gently in his left hand. With his right, he wove the ribbon around her slim wrists, tight enough that she couldn't free herself, not so tight that it cut into her skin. He tied the ends of the ribbon in a careful knot that hung gracefully from her bound wrists. When he looked at her again, she saw raw passion in his wide eyes. The liner that smudged his lower lids seemed to sweat and glow as he slowly raised her arms above her head with his left hand and picked up the strip of wood with his right. And when the music started, a lone sweet string melody, Shelly knew what it was that she had become.

The man drew his bow across her back, sliding perfect

symphonies against the silent strings tattooed into her skin. His eyes were closed, and his head was tilted back, and she could feel the power that lived inside of him. She could feel it in the grip of his left hand on her wrists and forearms, his swift fingers moving across her skin, pressing down on imaginary strings, moving in perfect time with the music that came from outside of them. She could feel it in the movement of his body as he swayed with the music, swayed with his music, around her body. She could feel it in his legs, firm with years of practice and performance, cradling her curved figure the way a musician held his favorite instrument. For the second time in her life, Shelly was unable to remove herself from her situation. His bow whipped back and forth, frenzied across the instrument that her body had become. She was enthralled by him, enraptured by his fervor, intoxicated by his music. Their music.

She didn't know how long she knelt there, a tool of passion between his knees. But when the music finally came to an end, the man simultaneously dropped his bow and her wrists, and his head sagged onto his chest, his breathing heavy and harsh. For several minutes, Shelly couldn't even move. She had never been used like this before, never felt so objectified in her entire life. But then again, wasn't her life with this man all she had ever known?

When he raised his head from his chest, the man's eyes were dull and empty once more. Drying streaks of wetness traced the skin from his eyes to his chin and he stared at her blankly, registering her presence with a blink. "Please go now." His voice had lost its tremor and its obvious restraint; he once again spoke softly through his heavy accent. "You will come to me again tomorrow."

Shelly stood up in one fluid motion, rocking back onto her toes and taking the weight off of her numb, forgiving knees. Head bowed with vulnerability and submission, she grabbed her pile of clothes from the floor and backed slowly out of the room, arms still tied at the wrists with the long brown ribbon. As soon as she heard his door click shut behind her, Shelly let the suppressed tears come forward. She was afraid of this man; a man who could lose himself so entirely to passion; a man who would use her in such an objectifying, terrifying, erotic way; a man who would vandalize her body for his own disturbing obsession.

She walked as quickly as she could without breaking into a run. She didn't know how good the man's hearing was, and she didn't want him to know how panicked she was. He seemed like the kind of man who played with power, and she didn't want to give him any more than he already had.

When she reached her room, which suddenly seemed suffocatingly large, she threw her clothes onto the loveseat and walked methodically towards her mirror. The mirror that he had planted in her room to taunt her, to tempt her, to distract her from her strong will. Unable to resist the compulsion any longer, Shelly turned her back to the mirror and stared at the terrible beauty that her spine had become.

What was once smooth skin had been transformed into a canvas for an artist's musical masterpiece. On the left side of her lower back, an S-shaped ribbon had been etched darkly into her skin. It was mirrored perfectly across the spine, creating a symmetrical design that she was sure represented artistic holes in the wooden instrument. From the base of her spine all the way up to her neck were four thin, parallel lines: C, G, D, and A, according to memories of music classes from a previous life. The skin of her back was raw from being scraped with the man's bow, his musical symphony etched out repulsively in jagged swipes across the new strings that she boasted.

A sudden wave of revulsion leapt up the back of her throat, overwhelming her fortitude, her numbness. She barely made it to the small garbage can beside her bed before her stomach evicted everything that it had been holding. After only a few seconds of vomiting food and bile, Shelly could only hold herself over the wastebasket and dry heave violently. She was vaguely aware of a gratitude for the ribbon that held her hair back in a tight bun.

Unable to breathe in the rancid odor of her own vomit any longer, Shelly made her shaky way over to her bed. When she fell onto the comforter, it seemed to consume her, too soft and too spongy to support her weight. She sank into the mattress, dreading the next day, and the day after that, and the day after that. This was her existence now. She belonged to the man for the rest of this life. And all of it—the skin-deep pain, the overwhelming bitterness, the obsessive symphony—all of it was so new to her.

The following days with the man were much like the first of his physical musical infatuation. Little by little, from the few words that he spoke, she learned pieces of the man's life. He had been a musician once, a famous cellist. Through him, she learned the specifics and technicalities of bowing a cello. It was rosin, he said, that actually made the sound when the bow scraped the strings. Without rosin on the bow, the strings would be unresponsive to its light touch. It was the rosin that really gripped, the rosin that created that friction, that sound. Not to worry, though. He wouldn't use rosin when he played her. Not unless she made him.

Though he was becoming more and more talkative as days passed, he became a single-minded machine as soon as the music began. Shelly was transformed into a mere instrument as soon as the first chord was strung. For hours he would scrape his bow across her strings, his fingers finding their places in perfect time with the melody.

Her back began to show lasting evidence of his musical escapades across her skin. Raised ridges crisscrossed the back of her rib cage, welting in a way that would take weeks of rest to heal. But he would never rest. He would never stop. For as long as he owned her, he would play her like the beautiful instrument that she was. "It's your shape…and your hair." She was his tool, his instrument, his cello. She belonged to him.

Shelly had always been good at numbing the pain. She had always been able to block out her surroundings, her situations, and the men who owned her. She had stayed disconnected from her world for so long that she had forgotten what it was like to be a part of it. But with this man, she found that she couldn't shut herself off from what he did to her. She was present at every moment of every symphony, every drag of the inked needle, every swipe of the unrosined bow. She had never been so present in her own body, in her own trauma. She had never been so unable to deal with her life. She had never been so desperate to escape.

Finally, when over a month had passed after her first interaction with the man and the artist and the whirring tattoo needle, Shelly knew she'd had enough. She needed to get out of this prison. She needed to escape from the man's insane obsession with her shape and her hair, his infatuation with the instrument into which she had been transformed. She waited until he was out—where, she didn't know, nor did she care—and slipped into his dark bedroom. The chill that always accompanied her entrance into his domain slipped in a familiar minor scale down her marked spine. Without wasting any time, she reached behind his straight-backed chair, his cellist's chair, and grabbed hold of the bow that had played her so fiercely. A token, she thought grimly, and focused her search onto that which she had never seen, but which had been described to her in such meticulous detail that she would recognize it as soon as it came before her eyes. And after only a few minutes of frantic rummaging, she found it: an amber bar, dusty from years of disuse. The rosin. The rosin that really gripped, the rosin that created that friction. The rosin that would save her from this orchestral hell that she had been living.

Carefully, meticulously, Shelly rosined the bow from tip to tip, scraping the brittle cake against the fine horsehairs that had so often caressed and abused her stained back. After thirty swipes with the bow—she had to be sure that the bow would really grip —she put the rosin back where she had found it and looked around the room with dull eyes, eyes that felt like the man's. She sat in his chair and immediately felt power wash through her. This was where the magic happened. This was where he tore down the strongest defenses any woman could ever have. This is where he made her feel pain and intoxication, all at once, in one destructive symphony. And this was where it would end.

Shelly positioned herself on the edge of the seat, legs spread to accommodate the imaginary cello that she intended to play. With a poise that she had seen in the man countless times, she lifted her left hand to grip the neck of her instrument and positioned her bow hand at the bridge. Her foot tapped the floor remote that controlled the stereo system, and a beautiful, sad symphony began.

It was slow and deep in the cello's heart, bringing tears to her eyes as she wove the bow back and forth over strings that she could not see and had never played. As her hands moved with the melody, she felt the ghost of the bow weeping across her back, engaging her entire body in this orchestral dance. The music built in intensity and fell, the tone ever deepening, the volume rising and falling with perfected crescendos and decrescendos. As the piece neared its climax, Shelly lost herself to the music. The rosined bow flew higher and higher up the neck of the imaginary cello, the chords becoming more forceful as her hands worked faster and faster. Finally, with a resonating crest of sound, the bow whipped across her neck in its final draw. The man had been right about the rosin—it really did grip.

In her final moments, as her breath came to her in ragged, bubbling gasps, she felt for the first time in all of her lives a moment of peace. It was finally over. This numbness was a gift, something that she couldn't control and didn't want to. She would never belong to anyone again. She would never be beaten, she would never be raped, she would never be tattooed and vandalized and used. She was no longer owned. She was no longer an object. She was no longer an instrument. All she would be from now on, Shelly thought, as she sat dying in his favorite chair, was a symbol.

Crane's Fire

A Daughter of Magic Story

Karen Eisenbrey

Crane was bursting to tell, but he couldn't. Not while Soorhi watched. The teacher might have been old as dirt, but he didn't miss much. Crane fidgeted. A breeze blew through the open windows. It smelled like apple blossoms. Like spring. Why were they inside on such a day? The eastern window framed a view of open country—grassland and rippling green wheat fields, broken here and there by splotches of purple or yellow where wildflowers bloomed. To the west lay the village of Deep River, though Crane could see only one house and part of another, built of gray river rock like the schoolhouse. Between them, he caught glimpses of a distant snow-capped mountain, and the dry gully that gave Deep River its name.

That was his whole world. But even on a beautiful day,

it could not distract from what Crane had to tell. The first chance he got, he would prove himself, and the others would have to accept him. Finally, he would belong. He drummed his fingers on the desk, waiting ...

The previous day, the big boys had lingered after school. They were old enough to have some responsibility now—chores and apprenticeships—but it was the first really warm day that spring. There had to be a better way to spend it. Rovhi, seventeen and done with school, had come on horseback to collect his younger brother, Huvro. They had farm work to do at home but got drawn into the huddle outside the school. Crane was part of the circle, yet outside it. At twelve, he was the youngest of this group, but already near in height to Rovhi.

"Let's do something!" Elic exclaimed. He raked his fingers through his curly brown hair, standing it up.

"Like what?" Breff asked. He was fourteen, a year older than Elic, but still deferred to him, as they all did—even Rovhi. They would do whatever he said. Even tolerate Crane.

"I don't know," Elic said. "No, wait, I do, too. Dares." He grinned.

The others welcomed this suggestion, but Crane almost left the group. He hated dares. On the rare occasion when he accepted a challenge, he failed, but he usually took the cowardly way out and refused the dare. Humiliating either way.

Elic met his gaze and gave him a little smile that said,

"Don't worry." It was always like that. Elic protected him and tried to build his confidence. Maybe, someday, it would work.

"Who's first?" Elic asked, but he'd already chosen. "Rovhi, you're oldest—show us how it's done." Rovhi nodded his assent. He stood tall and straightened his muscular shoulders. "Climb to the roof of the Village Hall and walk the length of the ridge."

"What, now?" Rovhi's face paled and his eyes darted nervously. He smoothed back his dark blond hair. For a moment, he looked like a young boy, in spite of his broad shoulders and sprouting beard.

"When I've finished all the challenges, we'll watch you," Elic replied. "Huvro, is there a bull in your pasture this spring?"

"Yes, a real snorter."

"Your challenge is to cross the bull's pasture...and he has to be in it."

Huvro swallowed visibly but nodded. He resembled his older brother but managed to respond more bravely to the dare. By this time, Rovhi had recovered himself. He laid a hand on Huvro's shoulder and grinned at Elic. "I'll make sure he does it."

"What about me?" Breff asked. He was a stocky, pale-haired farm boy, not a talker like Elic, but good-natured and up for anything.

"Yes, what about you?" Elic studied him. "I know. You will walk a girl home after school. Not a little girl; it has to be one our age, and she has to know you're walking her home. No following."

Breff blushed and grinned. "How—how will you know I did it?" he asked. Crane wondered about that, too. The girls attended school in the afternoon, when the boys would be with their masters or at work in the fields.

"Believe me, I'll know," Elic replied. They all laughed. Elic was close to Sunnea, a girl their age. If he asked, she would pass along news of anything that happened to any other girl in Deep River.

"Fine, I accept," Breff said. "But I get to give you yours: go inside the haunted house!"

"But that's not—" Crane began.

"I accept." Elic shot Crane a look that kept him quiet. "So, Rovhi?"

Crane couldn't believe his luck. Maybe he would get away without taking a challenge this time ...

"What about Crane?" Huvro asked.

Elic looked at Crane and shrugged. Crane stared back, only hoping that his friend would give him something that wasn't too humiliating. "I haven't forgotten," he said. "Crane gets the hardest one."

"What?" Crane protested.

Elic carried on as if he hadn't heard. "Crane, your challenge is to sneak into the Village Hall, into Jelf's library, and read some magic out of a spell-book."

The other boys gasped and stared at Crane, but he felt strangely calm. That didn't sound so hard, assuming the spell-books even existed. They were objects of mystery and dread, but Crane had never seen them; none of the boys had. Why there would be spell-books in Deep River—a place where nothing happened, let alone magic—was beyond Crane's imagining. But everyone knew they were there.

"I'll do it," Crane said. "But how will you know I succeeded?"

"Memorize a short spell and tell it to us tomorrow."

"What'll that prove?" Breff objected. "He should have to bring the book."

"I'm not stealing anything," Crane said.

"And we're not asking you to," Elic assured him. "Just tell us the spell. I doubt it will sound like anything we've heard before. Or that you could make up." He grinned at Crane. "Now, Rovhi, you have a challenge to meet."

They all accompanied Rovhi to the Village Hall, a long, low, building with walls of mortared river rock. Rovhi climbed at the nearest corner, using the many stones as hand- and foot-holds. It was an easier climb than Crane would have predicted. Once on the roof, Rovhi scrabbled on all fours up to the peak. The roof slates clanked and rattled under him. At the top, he stood. Crane held his breath and suspected he wasn't the only one. He had climbed the cottonwood tree behind the inn, but he'd never been on a rooftop. It must be like flying. Crane could fly…in his dreams. The dreams had begun recently, the best dreams he'd ever had. He hadn't shared them with anyone, not even Elic.

Rovhi took one slow, careful step after another, keeping his eyes fixed ahead of him. He never looked down. He wavered once or twice but didn't fall. When he reached the other end, he half-climbed, half-slid down the roof, then gripped the edge and swung down. He sank to his knees and rested his hands on the grass, pale and trembling.

At that moment, Jelf emerged from the Hall. He was a small man with thin brown hair going gray. Crane was surprised to see him, and from the look on his face, so was Elic. Jelf kept the village records but didn't usually start his work at the Hall until after lunch. It figured he'd have his meal early the one day he might get them into trouble. And it was only the first dare!

Jelf frowned at the boys. "Who's been on my roof?" he asked. He was not usually an intimidating figure, but today, he looked like a thunderhead. "I heard an awful racket up there just now."

"We didn't see anything. It must have been birds," Elic improvised.

"I didn't know birds could be that big and clumsy," Jelf said, eyeing Rovhi, who scrambled to his feet and joined the other boys. "I'm surprised none of you noticed them."

Crane, like the others, tried his best to look innocent. He wished he didn't have to lie to Jelf. He liked the old Keeper. It was bad enough that his own dare involved sneaking into the library.

"Well, don't you young men have anything better to do than stand in the road?" Jelf asked. "Get along!" He returned to the Hall without another word.

That was one dare down, and they weren't in trouble yet.

"That was close, huh?" Breff muttered to Crane, and grinned. "Good luck with yours."

Crane supposed it was only because he was closest, but for once, he felt really included. He smiled in agreement. With a wave of his hand, Breff set out on foot for home, a farm not far from town.

"Don't forget, you have to walk a girl home!" Elic called after him.

"I won't forget," he promised.

Rovhi and Huvro returned to the school and mounted the bay horse Rovhi had left tied there. They trotted past Crane and Elic. "I did it! Hoo-hoo!" Rovhi shouted. Huvro did not appear quite so lighthearted.

"That went well," Elic chuckled.

"What did you mean my dare was the hardest?" Crane asked.

"I thought it might get you some respect."

"So you lied?"

"Maybe not. You think any of them could do it? They're afraid of magic, but you've got more sense than that."

"It's not magic, it's books," Crane said. "So, no, I'm not afraid. But I could have done Rovhi's dare."

Elic chuckled. "I know. It would have been too easy for you. You'd have done it at a run! Rovhi's afraid of heights, but he'll do anything to save face. And Breff's shy, but he really does like girls, so his dare is just what he needs."

"Well, what if I like girls?" Crane asked.

"They won't speak to you," Elic said. "I can't change that."

That was true, though Crane didn't know why. Was it his freakish height? His dark skin? His straight black hair? All weak reasons, but what else was there? Maybe it was because the sky looked red to him, though he wasn't sure who knew about that. He hadn't mentioned it in a long time, since he saw how it upset his mother.

"Who wants to talk to girls, anyway?" he said. "They're stupid."

"Right," Elic agreed. "Stupid."

Elic didn't really think that, but it was nice to have his support. "What about yours?" Crane asked. "We both know that house isn't really haunted."

Elic shrugged. "Can I help it if Breff isn't as good at the game? Anyway, that makes it easier for me to help you."

"What makes you think I need help?"

"Not with your dare," Elic explained. "I'll just make sure you get inside."

"Jelf already suspects something," Crane said.

"Leave it to me." Elic grinned. He always relished a good trick. "Meet me at the Hall before sundown."

They parted at the Blue Heron Inn, Crane's home. Elic's

family lived across the road, and was like family to Crane. He called Elic's mother Aunt Sudi and Elic called Crane's mother Auntie Stell. Elic was his father's apprentice, though he had no particular aptitude for a blacksmith's work. Crane helped his mother with the inn, and expected to take it over someday. It wasn't a future he looked forward to, but it was the only one he had.

"Hello, Crane," she greeted him, peeking out of the kitchen. "How was school?"

"Same as always."

Mama was a small, pretty woman. She had wavy golden hair and a ready smile. She and Crane shared the same hazel eye color, but there the resemblance ended. Crane had often wondered about that. Everyone he knew looked like their parents or other relatives. If he didn't look like his mother, then he must look like his father—whoever that was. Like wings, a father was something Crane had only in dreams.

They sat down to lunch. Crane ate a few bites of his bean soup, then put down his spoon. "Who was my father?"

Mama stared at him and didn't answer right away. "Haven't you learned, there's nothing to be gained in asking that?" she said at last. "He's gone far away, and he won't be back."

When Crane was younger and asked that question, she told stories. They didn't answer his question, but he liked hearing them. He waited, but she said no more. They both ate lunch in silence. He's gone far away, and he won't be back. Did that mean he was dead? There was no other way to be so sure he wouldn't return. His father was dead, and Crane would never know any more about him.

Chores filled the afternoon, and Crane soon forgot his question. He pumped water, weeded the vegetable garden, fed the chickens, and cleaned the upstairs rooms. He tried to remember the last time someone had come to stay. He couldn't, but Mama insisted the rooms be clean, just in case.

Although the sleeping rooms remained empty, they could be sure the common room wouldn't. Most of the men in Deep River and from the surrounding farms liked to enjoy a mug of ale and a few stories at the Blue Heron at least once of week. The unmarried men took most of their suppers there. Crane ate his own supper early so he could help serve but kept an eye on the waning daylight.

"I have to meet Elic for a little while," he said.

"Now? What for?" Mama asked.

"It's—for school," he replied. "We have to talk to Jelf at the Hall."

"Why didn't you do it right after school?"

"Elic couldn't stay," Crane said. "It shouldn't take long. I'll be back as soon as I can." He whisked out the door before she could say anything more. He hadn't quite lied, and if they didn't get caught, he wouldn't have to.

With the low sun behind him, Crane's shadow stretched out in front of him halfway to the Village Hall.

The sunset seemed to fill the whole sky. Even the east was tinted purple and dark red. Crane liked the light of sunrise and sunset best, when the sky really was red. Then he didn't have to work to see the blue beyond the shimmering red net no one else could see.

As Crane approached the Hall, Elic emerged from the shadows at the far end and beckoned to him.

"You wait here, out of sight," he whispered. "I'll try to distract Jelf before he locks up. Slip in as soon as you can."

Crane crouched in the shadows and watched Elic trot up the road toward the school and Soorhi's house. He circled around and walked back. When the door of the Hall opened, he broke into a run.

"Jelf! I'm glad I caught you," he called.

The old man turned toward him, the key in his hand. "Elic? What is it?"

"A strange plant sprouted in Soorhi's garden," Elic said. "Soorhi says it's edible, but Mam says it's poisonous. Soorhi wants your opinion."

Jelf chuckled. "I don't know what I can add to their knowledge, but I'll take a look. Lead on!"

Elic and Jelf headed back toward Soorhi's. Crane shrank further into the shadows, though Elic's description of the mystery plant held Jelf's attention as they passed. As soon as it seemed safe, he darted out of hiding and up to the door. He pushed, and it opened—still unlocked. He closed it behind him.

He paused in the dim Hall to let his eyes adjust, then

crept past the long meeting table and chairs, toward a smaller room at the end. This door didn't have a lock. He pushed in and approached the shelves. The upper shelves held logs and registers, in which Jelf kept track of village events. The bottom shelf was in shadow.

He crouched down. He could discern a row of books—four thick ones with dark covers, along with a few thinner volumes. They were all coated in dust, and in the poor light, Crane couldn't tell whether or not there were any words on the spines. The last of the sunset light filtered in through the closed shutters. Crane didn't know how he would manage to read anything, but he didn't dare light a lamp and give himself away. He would just have to hurry and finish the job before the light failed completely.

He grabbed one of the big books at random. His whole arm tingled as if he'd banged his elbow, and he dropped the book. Dust puffed in his face, and he sneezed twice. He froze, certain the whole village had heard. But the evening quiet went on, undisturbed. He picked up the book. This time, his arm did not tingle, but he had a brief impression of a pale, dark-haired man with a fierce expression. Maybe there was something magical about the book. He carried it to Jelf's desk, where the light was a little better. The dark red leather binding bore no words or marks of any kind.

Crane let the book fall open and stared at the yellowed page. Disappointment rose like bile in his throat. He couldn't read it. There were letters and even syllables that looked familiar, but nothing on the page made sense. He was about to close the book and give up, when the letters and syllables flickered like candlelight before his eyes and rearranged themselves. They still didn't look like familiar words, but he knew they had meaning.

Crane chose a short, two-word spell—he hoped it was a spell—and committed it to memory. It felt strange to memorize something he didn't understand. He had to guess at the pronunciation, though he didn't dare speak aloud in case anyone should hear. But none of the other boys would be able to correct him, so perhaps it didn't matter how he pronounced the words, as long as he told them something.

As he returned the book to its place on the shelf, he froze at the sound of voices.

"I don't know what you were thinking, bothering me about a potato plant!" Jelf said.

"I didn't know that's what it was," Elic replied. "I never saw the plant before, just the spud."

The voices drew nearer, and Crane feared Jelf would come into the Hall. Or what if he locked the door, with Crane still inside?

"Perhaps Soorhi and your mother have played a joke on you, then. It's no more than you deserve, after all your tricks."

"That must be it. You're not angry, are you?"

It sounded like they'd stopped at the corner of the Hall, where the path to Jelf's house met the road. Crane relaxed.

Maybe he wouldn't get caught, after all.

"Of course not," Jelf said. "Sometimes doing something foolish is the only way to learn. Good night, Elic."

Elic's laughter rang through the village. "Good night, Jelf!"

Crane waited a moment longer to give Jelf time to reach home, then scurried out of the Village Hall and back to the inn. He'd done something right! He'd accepted and fulfilled a dare. But there was no time to celebrate now. It was suppertime at the Blue Heron, and Mama needed his help. He took a deep breath to calm himself and pushed open the door. The common room was bright with lamplight and noisy with supper guests.

"That didn't take long," Mama said. She handed him his apron.

"It didn't?" It seemed an age had passed since he left for the Hall. "No, I guess it didn't."

"Did you find what you needed?"

"Um—yes," he replied, tying the apron. "So, what needs doing?"

* * *

Crane hurried to school in the morning, excited to prove his daring. Elic was already there ahead of him, waiting outside.

"Did you do it?" he asked.

"Yes!" Crane exclaimed. "The books are really there. I—"

Rovhi and Huvro arrived then, interrupting Crane. Huvro slid off the horse to join them.

"Huvro's braver than I thought," Rovhi called down. "He did exactly what you asked and lived to tell about it."

"That bull knows me," Huvro whispered to Elic.

"It doesn't matter. You fulfilled the dare."

As Rovhi rode away, Breff joined them, pink in the face from his long walk. "I did it!" he announced. "I waited for the girls to get out of school and asked Kiat if I could walk her home!"

"And what did she say?" Elic asked.

Breff turned a brighter pink. "She told me to jump in the river."

They all laughed. Anyone who jumped in that dry gully was more likely to break a leg than drown. Crane had often wondered why they still called it a river, when it had been dry since before he was born, but no one else seemed to give it much thought.

"That doesn't sound like a very promising conversation," Elic observed.

"No, not really," Breff admitted. "Except then, Tiek said I could walk her home." He grinned. Tiek was Kiat's twin sister. They looked similar, but they couldn't have been more different in temperament.

"Well done, Breff! That's three completed," Elic said. "I haven't done mine yet. We should all go to the haunted house right after school."

"What about Crane?" Breff asked.

Before he could answer, Soorhi came outside. The morning sun lit his white hair like a bright cloud. "I don't see what's so amusing out here," he said, "but it's time to come inside."

They filed in and took their places. Crane had the middle seat, with Elic on his right and Breff on his left. Huvro sat behind Breff, while the ten-year-olds Lafa and Alryg sat in the front row. Crane was bursting to tell about his dare, but he couldn't while Soorhi watched. The first chance he got, he would prove that he'd fulfilled the challenge, and they'd have to accept him fully. He drummed his fingers on the desk, waiting.

As soon as Soorhi's back was turned, Elic and Breff leaned in. "Tell us!" they whispered. Huvro half stood to get into the conversation.

Crane balled his hands into fists. He couldn't afford to forget what he'd read. He closed his eyes and the page appeared in memory, flickering like candlelight. He took a deep breath and whispered the words, reading them off the imagined page. There was no question now about pronunciation. His voice sounded strange to him, crackling with a new energy.

Elic yelled, and from the thud, it sounded like Breff had fallen out of his seat. Crane opened his eyes. His right hand was in flames. He stared at it, unable to make a sound. The other boys drew back, horror-stricken. Only Elic stayed close. "It wasn't supposed to do anything," he whispered.

Through the flames, Crane saw Soorhi vault over his desk with the energy of a man a quarter his age. The teacher came straight to Crane and smothered the flames with his bare hands.

The whole event took only a moment. Now that the panic was over, Crane expected they would all take their seats again and go on with class as usual. He would never hear the end of this! Then the pain struck him. He thought his hand must have burned off, except that he could feel each finger alive with agony. He didn't dare look. He fainted.

He had no idea how much time had passed when he came to. Probably not much—it was still daylight. Or had days passed? He lay in his own bed. Someone had bandaged his hand. It rested on a pillow on top of the covers. The pain was a little less, though still enough to bring tears to his eyes. He thought he might faint again—he wished he could—but remained conscious. Several people stood just inside his room, talking together in low tones: his mother, Aunt Sudi, and Soorhi.

"I put a salve on it, but it's going to scar," Sudi said.

"Badly?" Mama asked.

"I can't tell yet," Sudi said. "It could be pretty bad. From what Soorhi tells me, we're lucky he didn't lose his whole hand."

Mama sobbed once, then controlled herself. "How did it happen?"

"I think he said a fire spell, but how could he have

learned such a thing?" Soorhi said.

"A fire spell?" Mama repeated. "You mean, magic?"

"Yes," Soorhi said. "You have a budding wizard on your hands."

"He chose a fine way to let us know," Sudi snapped.

"I don't think he had any idea," Soorhi said. "But where did he learn the spell?"

"Doesn't Jelf have some old spell-books at the Village Hall?" Sudi asked. "You remember, that some old wizard left behind?"

Soorhi was silent a moment. "Lok's books. Yes. Could Crane have seen them?"

"He said he was meeting Elic at the Hall last night," Mama said. "I shouldn't have let him go!"

"It wasn't your fault," Soorhi assured her. "I'm going to see if Jelf knows anything about this. It might be best to let Crane study those books openly. Otherwise, he could be a danger to himself or others."

Crane heard one set of footsteps cross the common room and leave the inn. Had he heard right? A danger? To himself, certainly. But to others? He wouldn't let that happen. They had nothing to fear from him. But he remembered how the other boys had drawn away from him.

"Will he be able to use that hand?" Mama asked. "Are you sure it won't heal without scarring?"

"I'm sorry, Stell," Sudi said. "There's only so much I can do."

Mama moved to the bedside. Crane closed his eyes, feigning sleep. "If only his father would come," she whispered, so low that Crane doubted Sudi had heard. It seemed an odd thing to say. Wasn't his father dead? Did she think Crane was going to die? But he was more interested in what Soorhi had said. He could be a wizard! He didn't have to be an innkeeper. He could study the magic in those books and find something he was actually good at. Was that what the red sky meant? That there was magic in Deep River, in him? If he could make fire, then he could do anything—bring rain, cure sickness, change his own form. Fly.

His hand throbbed, but it was worth it. It would be easy. He drifted off to sleep and dreamed he had wings.

The Woman Against the Window

Rosie Bueford

Sarah searched row by row for her seat. The crowded plane was a circus of people trying to get to their seats. People pushed past each other in an aisle that already felt half-a-human size, then awkwardly tucked into their rows to let others by while still trying to thrust their bags up into the bins above. She had thought most of the chaos would have died down by waiting to be one of the last to board. It hadn't. People took way too much time to shuffle, shove and shimmy into their seats, apparently.

For the first time ever, she wasn't overloaded with luggage, though. She had one medium-sized tote and a book. She was going to have the most comfortable flight because there was nothing heavy weighing her down. No baggage to try and stuff in an overhead compartment while nearly climbing on a seatmate's lap. No giant, overstuffed purse to share legroom with. This short flight was going to be the easiest, the breeziest.

Ticket clutched in hand, her eyes compared the scribbled alphanumeric code on her ticket to the signage above the rows of seats. Locating her seatmate was always like a game of "Stranger Roulette," the "How Awkward or Normal" edition. She'd been stuck next to all kinds of neighbors. Some wreaking of B.O. to the point of nausea, some so pleasant and interesting she left the pressurized cabin feeling rejuvenated and inspired. Some people were obnoxious, some slept, some snored, and some surfed a mind-numbing amount of social media on their bright LED phone screens. Flying was rarely a joy, and, arguably, learning to share the cramped area was an integral part of being able to survive the ride. You couldn't shift your back out of a stinky neighbor. You couldn't stretch your legs long enough to escape an endless talker.

Upon finding her seat, her eyes went immediately to study the occupants of the seats next to her. A slender, petite woman sat against the window hidden by a man draped over her. He wasn't much larger than her, so it wasn't his size that nearly blocked her from sight. It was *how* he was flung, limbs and all, cloaked over her like a blanket. It appeared quite uncomfortable, mainly for her, but even for him. It just didn't look like the normal position two love birds would assume when preparing for a late-night flight, sleeping or not. Regardless, she noted the plus side: *At least there is no question, I have both armrests to myself.*

Sarah slid smoothly down into her seat with the greatest amount of grace she'd ever displayed on an airline. There was almost an incomplete feeling to the ease of the thing. She buckled her seatbelt and prepared to fully immerse herself into the book she brought.

As the aisle cleared of travelers, flight attendants stomped with purpose up and down the aisle, preparing for takeoff or doing whatever it was that flight attendants did during the lull between frantic boarding and lifting into the air. She breathed a sigh of relief and opened her book.

"Put your seatbelt on. You need to. Hey!" The matronly sounding commands were met with exasperated heavy breaths from the squished woman against the window. The slumped man didn't respond. The flight attendant issued a grunt of annoyance. Her small hands reached around the seemingly unconscious man to search blindly for the seat belt ends. She was surprisingly successful, buckling him in to safety.

Is this moron drunk? Sarah wondered, pausing from her reading to judge the situation from her peripheral. For Sarah, the incident left an odd sense of annoyance in the air.

* * *

A muffled voice came over the airline intercom to announce the flight time, cruising altitude, and expected smooth travel. The lights dimmed, and the seatbelt-fasten signs turned off with a pleasant ding. A momentary worry crossed Sarah's mind about whether or not it would be inconsiderate to turn her reading light on, but one glance at her entangled neighbors brushed the notion aside. She clicked it on and continued her reading.

Sarah had turned a few pages of her book when the man next to her showed the first sign of life since boarding by uttering a long, throaty groan. It was more of a wet hack and extended grunt combination, which sounded rather disgusting.

Is he going to throw up? Her anxious curiosity was purely motivated by selfishness. She hated puke. Like, *really* hated puke. Even worse, the thought of having to scramble away from puke in an already cramped area created a stirring panic. He shifted his body further onto his girlfriend, or whatever she was to him, pushing her further against the window. She grimaced instantly but resituated her head against the window, pretending to ignore the discomfort he was causing her. Sarah hoped her face wasn't involuntarily displaying her judgement and annoyance.

More shifting. More odd groaning. Reading became more and more difficult with the untimely interruptions. She had, with utmost certainty, made up her mind that he was drunk. This wasn't necessarily a problem, but then…Then she noticed a new maneuver from the inebriated oaf. A maneuver he was not even trying to be inconspicuous about.

His arm had reached into the woman's skirt, deep in

between his partner's legs, and was aggressively thrusting. His elbow, obviously jutted outward, had caught her eye. The rhythmic twitching of his muscles was unmistakable.

You've got to be fucking kidding me, Sarah groaned inwardly. She knew her facial expressions couldn't be hidden this time. Shock involuntarily bolted from her eyes as her eyebrows raised. But she had no travel buddy to share the look with. No one to sympathize with her newly developing problem. Her eyes tried to focus on the words of her book, but her brain couldn't organize them into recognizable sentences. She was just staring at the page, heart racing, trying to figure out how best to handle this awkward predicament. She couldn't decide if she was annoyed at the couple's lack of courtesy or offended by the shameless behavior of the drunk man.

Oddly, the woman against the window seemed unmoved by the man's touch. Her head was still laid against the window, mostly turned away from him, her eyes closed as if she were sleeping.

Should I turn this light off? Give them some privacy? God no! Don't encourage it further! Her internal argument heightened her anxiety as she tried to determine what to do to lessen the awkwardness. She often argued with herself but hoped her face hid the emotions of the back and forth commentary.

She wasn't a prude; sexual expression wasn't something that normally rattled her. For all it was worth, she was certain she had done some things in public that would have made others uncomfortable a time or two. This seemed a bit different, though. Maybe because Sarah presumed he was drunk? Or because she couldn't scoot away to a more comfortable distance? Did it bug her that the woman seemed to ignore the situation completely, as if she wasn't participating in the act?

The thrusting, the huffs of breath from the man, his slumped suffocating body all made Sarah feel claustrophobic. She wanted this to be over. *Should I tell someone? Haha. Sure. And then what? It's a full flight*. Sarah's sarcastic nature came out even in her thoughts. *You're stuck. So, try to read and ignore them.*

Sarah stared at the book, wishing she could lose herself in the story and be done with the growing knot in her stomach. She adjusted her seat belt. Somehow it seemed tighter than when she first put it on. She felt so *uncool* all of sudden. Maybe this was something people did now on airplanes. Maybe she was the one being too nosy, and she needed to *just be cool, Sarah.*

An abrupt motion from the woman's hand seized the man's muscles and halted the rhythm he had been maintaining. She grabbed his hand and held it tightly, placing their finger entanglement upon her lap. Sarah noticed her strained fingers, white knuckles. She placed her other hand on top seeming to reinforce her demand to "stop!"

Sarah exhaled the pent-up tension she had been

holding in her chest.

She sat as still as possible, unable to settle from the previous scene. Maybe if both her and the woman against the window didn't disturb the man, he would choose sleep and not attempt any other offensive or obnoxious pastimes. Maybe then she could read for the rest of the flight. Maybe then the sick feeling deep in her gut would go away. Maybe then…

Sarah's thoughts were turning into a mantra. Something to focus on so that time would keep ticking forward, and as it ticked things would stay peaceful. Manageable at the very least. Her focus was shattered by a loud, uninhibited sneeze by the man next to her. Followed by another. He did nothing to cover his sneeze, spewing whatever bodily fluids he had directly on to his partner's bare chest and shoulders. Her low hanging tank top probably allowed his drool to run right in between her breasts.

How disgusting. Sarah shuddered. His partner stayed still. He coughed and hacked a few times as well, right onto the woman. Sarah's face purposely contorted into a show of revulsion. Sarah now couldn't decide which bugged her more—the lack of respect this guy was displaying toward the woman against the window or the level of disrespect this woman appeared to passively allow. *Who lets someone treat them like this? Is she drunk too?*

The knot in Sarah's stomach was twisting its way up into her chest and throat. Warping into new worries, new questions, new assessments of what was happening. The man let out a very deep, throaty hack, similar to earlier. *Will he nonchalantly throw up on this woman, too? Will she allow it like she's allowed everything else?*

The utterance seemed to force the man's body to sprawl out across the entire group of seats. His torso shoved harder onto his partner, while his legs spread and pushed against Sarah's leg. His foot shoved Sarah's bag and foot aside. His repulsive intrusion into Sarah's space caused her to recoil, trying to avoid his touch on every level.

Just try to stay out of his way, Sarah told herself as she scooted her bag farther over, trying to free up a bit more leg room for herself. *At least this is better than what was happening earlier.* Sarah accepted that he was now taking over her area too. She felt a bit of defeat as she re-opened her book. The defeat didn't sit well with her though.

Why should she let him push her around, too? *Why does he get to take over the entire row and command use of everything and everyone in his way? Why?* She could *not,* on a very principled level, allow him to be so inconsiderate. Sarah decided.

She shut her book with a motivated snap, alighting her dimmed confidence. She shoved her foot against his, hoping to push him back into his own designated space. He didn't budge. Sarah wasn't looking to do something too bold. But she felt it necessary to establish he couldn't push her around like he did the woman against the window. Sarah was *not* his. She prepared herself to put more *umph* into her exertion and forcibly shoved his foot and leg back to their seat. A minor victory, but the hint of strength gave Sarah a resolved feeling. She set a boundary. She took back her spot. She wished the tiny woman against the window would do the same.

It bothered Sarah to watch this woman accept this man's selfishness. How could she allow him to use her body in so many ways so thoughtlessly? Her body, her humanness, was not a utility to service his every need or desire. Why did this entire scene seem to be so…Sarah couldn't find the word she was looking for, but the vibe she got felt gross. A slimy, shady version of abuse too indistinct to label, too discrete to call out.

Within minutes of Sarah's act of strength, the man began stirring. His hand had slipped from the woman's lap and disappeared up her skirt. The woman, as small as she was, sat with her legs drawn up onto the seat. "Crisscross applesauce" as Sarah's niece called it. Sarah's gut instantly re-tightened. Her head felt light.

Damn it. I should have never moved. Sarah blamed her stupid boundary setting battle for the man's return to violating his sleeping mate. She no longer felt like the small victory was worth it. Had she been given a choice, she would have kept the cramped leg room. Sarah caught herself holding her breath. It took forced, concentrated decisions to inhale and exhale. In and out. Her breaths methodical, deeply rhythmic. Unlike the aggressive rooting the man was doing with his hand.

His jerky and chaotic movements proved one of two things. He knew nothing about how to please a woman, or he cared nothing of pleasing this woman. Likely, both. He didn't come across as a suave Casanova. Sarah had not seen his face the entire flight, but she pictured a narcissistic smile trying to hide clumsy lips and slightly crooked teeth. An overly confident stare from bloodshot eyes. He wasn't dressed fashionably. Faded black t-shirt and stupid baggy pants. Zipper down.

Dear God. Sarah near gagged upon noticing his agape zipper. *If I see his dick, I swear I will…* She wanted to make up some bold threat in her mind, but she stopped. She felt powerless. She couldn't even feign bravery to her own self. *What, Sarah? What are you going to do? You haven't been confident enough to do anything this far, how would a hard dick change things?*

She was angry at herself for not knowing how to deal with this. She was angry that she didn't even know how standing up for what's right would look like here. *Is there a right or wrong here?* She was even more angry at the woman who seemed to act like this was just another Sunday afternoon flight where her man needed a moment to grapple with her lady parts like he needed a tissue to blow his nose on. Snatch, use, discard.

The woman shifted her body, grabbing the man's hand, firmly placing it back on her lap. A harsh, indiscernible whisper was uttered to the man. Sarah assumed the woman was putting a more final end to the man's behavior. Whatever the woman had said didn't work, though. The man dug his face into her bosom and returned his hand to his preferred place beneath her skirt. The woman rolled her eyes and turned her head back to sleep against the window.

Sarah's anger mounted with every breath she was forcing herself to take. Of the three of them, who should she blame most for what was continuing to happen? Was it the drunk asshole who, all in one flight, had used this woman as his human pillow, his sex toy, his sneeze and cough cover, and his safety-belt buckler? Or was it the woman against the window wearing a skirt, sitting in the most vulnerable position, providing no obstacle for her own exploitation? Sarah wondered if she even wore panties. And what about Sarah? Cowardly, confused Sarah.

Whose fault was this?

Sarah tried to stop her mind from spinning out on a tirade. She hated that she blamed the woman for how she sat and what she wore. She hated that this entire scenario was exposing her own personal weaknesses and insecurities. Even if his overall intrusions were toward the woman against the window, his overbearing presence seemed to command something from Sarah, too.

Sarah adjusted her seat belt again, trying to loosen it more. She fluffed her shirt slightly to readjust how it laid against the curves of her body. Her body felt awkward and frumpy all of a sudden. She noticed a small stain on her jeans. It added to the swelling pressure pushing against her lungs. It added to the fog dizzying her brain. Her hands were clammy which, in Sarah's experience, meant soon she would be dealing with embarrassing pit stains from the uncontrollable sweat. She wanted to shift her weight, turn on the air above her, but her body was paralyzed. Her fear, her anger, her embarrassment all told her that any movement from her would just worsen the situation. Why did Sarah feel like a victim when the woman against the window was the one getting molested by this carnal drunkard?

An obscene amount of time later, the woman against the window finally had enough. She straightened her body up. Stiff. Purposed. She brought her legs down, forcing the man's arm away. She crossed her legs and issued another stern, indistinguishable command to the man. Sarah realized it wasn't the low toned whisper that scrambled the words, but that the woman wasn't speaking English.

Sarah was glad to see the woman emboldened. The woman against the window must have finally awakened her courage. *About time,* Sarah wanted to passively aggressively whisper. For some reason, Sarah wanted the woman to know how annoyed she was at her. She wanted the woman to know she was allowing something so much bigger than just her little moment on the plane. She was allowing a lifetime of slavery. Sarah toggled between wishing to encourage her and wishing to scold her.

You are so much more than this, Sarah wanted her to know. She wanted to know why she didn't already know. The annoyance and anger toward the woman against the window was transforming into a deep desire to save her from whatever it was that was trapping her. Sarah didn't want to judge this woman, she wanted to help her.

It's never too late to stand up for yourself. Sarah reminded herself of that, too. Sarah was there, in that moment, too. Sarah had also been in previous moments where she didn't stand up. She had rolled her eyes and succumbed before. This wasn't just the woman against the window's heavy baggage. This was Sarah's baggage, too. And the woman's sitting six rows forward. It was Sarah's four-year-old niece's weight to carry, even. It was, honestly, every woman's weight.

Sarah's mental soap box was knocked from under her feet as the clumsy chump sprawled back out, tipping over Sarah's tote. Her wallet and cosmetic wristlet tumbled out of the tote into the aisle. Sarah's previous paralysis had subsided from the empowering internal rant. She scrambled to get the items, no longer worrying if her movements would disrupt the current state. The jostling startled the woman against the window. For the first time, Sarah saw the woman's face—her engaged, open eyes.

Sarah looked into them. *Quick, what facial expression will tell her everything she should know right now?* Sarah's brain searched its muscle memory log for the most meaningful, powerful look it had. Unfortunately, in return, the woman looked at Sarah and apologized for the man. She wrapped her arms around the man and tried to pull his body closer to her. He didn't budge. She grabbed his pant leg and tried to pull his legs away from Sarah, still apologizing. The man finally complied with the woman's tugs, moving away from Sarah's area. The woman mouthed one last apology before resigning back to her usual posture against the window. She now had her arm around the man's shoulders as he slumped deeper onto her torso and lap. She embraced him the rest of the flight.

That was it. The woman apologized for the man. She stood up for *him*. She let a drunk, ignorant bastard reduce her to a spokeswoman covering for his awful behavior. Sarah wondered what the woman's internal conversation was to herself. Was she making excuses? Did she believe he was worth standing up for? Was she defeated? Was she happy? Sarah wondered if the woman felt as enslaved as she appeared to be from the outside.

How, though? How could someone walk away from being used in so many ways and still have dignity? Was there a way to allow such reckless treatment of one's self and still have confidence? Sarah was back to wondering if she should do something to empower this woman. To remind her she was a woman of worth.

The sick feeling in Sarah's stomach was melting into a heavy sludge that left a lingering bout of nausea. This easy breezy flight had turned into the heaviest. Sarah's shoulders slouched. Her eyes were tired and weary. She still didn't know what to do. Maybe she shouldn't do anything. Maybe this was just part of life; sometimes you were a fly on the wall of another's story, doing nothing but watching and learning. But…that resignation didn't give Sarah the closure she needed. There was more. There had to be. As a woman. As a daughter. As a friend. As a future mother of daughters.

Sarah wondered what her mother would have done in that moment. Sarah's mom, a fiery, stocky woman, wouldn't have let this scene unfold the way Sarah had allowed it to. She would have approached it with a grace and tenacity Sarah wished she had. Sarah was raised to *stand up*. She could hear her mother's deep, smooth voice speaking the words as she thought them. Sarah saw her single, hard working mama conquer the world.

But even with a role model like that raising her, Sarah found the real world a much harder place to be so bold. Somehow, Mother wasn't intimidated by the world. She wasn't put in a corner or a box or a kitchen. Sarah admired her for her ability to exquisitely *stand up*. But, Sarah didn't have it. Sarah possessed strength in bouts. She had her ideals. But this moment was a shining example of Sarah's own indecisive, intimidated self.

It was proof that even with the most beautiful, strong mother, a woman can fall. A woman can forget how to *stand up*. Sarah found herself feeling guilty for not being more like her mother. Her thoughts trickled into wondering about the woman against the window and what kind of mother she had. Maybe her mom was stuck in a kitchen serving a man quite similar to the brute that was flung across her lap.

It didn't really matter what Sarah's mama was like, or what this woman's mama was like. What mattered was here they were. Sarah and the woman against the window. Being women on a plane where the implication was that there was nothing they could do to *stand up*.

I wonder if this bastard would have been so audacious if a man had sat in my place? Would the woman against the window have been free of all these invasions if a man had been here instead? The realization broke her spirit. Sarah's lip quivered. She sighed a breath of helplessness.

The *bump, jerk, jolt* of the wheels hitting the ground made Sarah awaken from her thoughts and their wandering path. She had been so consumed with trying to sort through the layers of everything that was occurring, she didn't even realize the flight was over. Her wish was being granted. It was over. *This* was over.

The plane made the short taxi to the terminal, and before Sarah could ponder, contemplate, debate or any other sort of internal reasoning, she grabbed her light, easy-to-carry tote and book to make her easy, breezy escape. She slid out of her seat with as much ease as she had entered. She chose not to look at the woman. She chose not to do anything.

She chose to run. She ran through the terminal.

Through the parking garage. To sit in her car. And cry. She wondered if the woman against the window would cry that night, too. Or not. And which was sadder?

The Painted Ponies of Wiley Creek

Elizabeth Beechwood

Every now and again, the men of Carbondale, when they got themselves all riled up and drunk, would declare that they was goin' out and gettin' themselves a Painted Pony. They'd clamber up on their horses and shoot up the moon and thunder off into the desert, nearly falling out of their saddles. In the morning, they'd come crawling back with headaches and stories 'bout seeing the sparks of silver hooves in the dark and swearin' they'd heard laughter and piano music echoing through the canyons. Once, Three-Toed Joe woke up in the middle of town with a hoof print on his forehead and no memories of the past three days as proof of such things.

On those mornings, Madame Pearl Wiley would stand on the balcony of her fine establishment on Main Street, on the opposite end of town from the First Church of Christ the Cowboy, and watch the men crawl off to their beds. She'd shake her head, then shake out the sheets, clean out the secrets and lies, and give her gals the afternoon off. She'd harness her fine bay filly to her fine black carriage and drive on out to her place—a five hundred acre spread that many a man had offered to marry her for.

Pearl Wiley had no use for men in general, discovering long ago that taking her own needs in hand was far cheaper than taking another husband. Her first and only husband, God rest his soul, had had the good sense to die quickly in a duel over something stupid. She, being the sole inheritor, had liquefied his assets and headed off toward the setting sun.

* * *

"Can you smell it, Bunny?" The words tore out of Clara's throat like a cactus paddle. "Can you smell the water?"

Clara dug her elbow into the sandstone dust and wrenched around to find Bunny. But her little gray mare wasn't there. She hadn't been for three days now. Clara kept forgetting that.

They were supposed to be going to California together. To be a gentleman rancher and his retired cowpony. There wasn't much point in crawling any further without Bunny. But the desire to survive wasn't letting go of Clara so easily. She hauled herself up the bluff with fingernails bleeding and skin scraping dirt and rock. Her clothes had shredded some time during the past two days but, luckily, the thick cotton bandages that bound her breasts were fairly intact. Clara figured it was only fitting that the fabric that hid her unfortunate sex would also provide some protection.

The sun was dropping toward late afternoon. Soon, night would bring some relief from the heat. But then the cold would come descending like a mountain lion. Clara groaned deep in her heart and pulled herself up to the edge of the bluff.

What she saw surely could not exist.

Perhaps she was delirious with thirst.

Before her lay a long valley, appearing out of nowhere in the south and disappearing into buttes in the north. It was narrow, only an hour's ride across on a good pony. But it wasn't the valley itself that seemed unreal. Clara'd ridden through plenty of them in her ten years moving cattle. This valley had a stripe of green grass running down its middle, like the line down a burro's back. There were even a few cottonwoods standing in a crooked line.

"There's a creek down there," she told Bunny. She said 'creek' like her mama had taught her, back when she was little Clarabelle Cariveau, living in Boston. Not 'crick' like she'd come to say as Clark Smith. Mama'd be proud. Maybe. Her mother was a dream, a wish. Bunny, poor Bunny with buzzards tearing out her insides because Clara had thought they could outrun a damn sandstorm, was more real to her than her mother. She ran her arm across her forehead, swiping at sweat, flies, and memories.

There was a nicker. Then a whinny. Then the mighty thunder of hooves shook the ground. Clara turned quick as her poor body could manage as the ponies came on her. No blacks or browns or greys among them—in skins of cobalt, orange, chartreuse, emerald, yellow, they pirouetted between rattlesnakes and gopher holes on gold and silver hooves. Their manes and tails flew like standards declaring freedom. They were as beautiful and tough as desert flowers and led by a stocky scarlet mare with bells jingling in her mane. And they were all running straight at Clara.

Startled that her death would come so quickly after so much suffering, Clara rolled to her stomach, covered her head with her arms, and counted down how much longer she had…three…two…one…

But instead of trampling her, the lead mare dodged right at the last minute and the river of ponies flowed around her, leaping over the edge of the butte. After the last pony passed her by, she looked down into the valley where the ponies danced in the green grass.

Their story was told around every campfire from Alberta to Abilene. The details changed some, depending on the teller, but one fact remained unchanged—the Painted Ponies danced along Wiley Creek.

The lead mare broke away from the herd and stared up at Clara. Clara's fingers twitched with the urge to grab a rope and lasso the mare, to climb onto her back and ride all the way to California. Or at least let the mare drag her to the creek hidden somewhere in the grass. The mare scratched at the ground with a silver hoof. She lowered her head and snorted. Clara heard the challenge as if the mare had spoken to her—Catch me if you can!

"You're a sly one," Clara croaked. "Even if I did have my rope, you know I don't have the strength to catch you."

The lead mare tossed her head. Yes, she surely knew.

Clara screamed, low and loud, as she hauled herself up and over, slid down, and tumbled to the valley floor. She crawled until her fingers sank into damp ground and her belly was stained green, until her short brown hair was slick with water. She sucked Wiley Creek down her throat.

The cold settled in, and Clara's teeth began to chatter.

Maybe the night would accomplish what the blazing day could not.

"Oh, fuck me," Clara said as that last bit of struggling to survive whispered away. They were coarse last words, to be sure, but they seemed appropriate.

There was a rustle in the grasses. Too small to be a pony. A coyote or wolf then. Life was full of surprises.

Then a woman's voice drawled, "What do you have, Poppy?"

A face appeared above Clara: silver hair, crystal blue eyes, skin impossibly white in this desert—maybe it had been darker once and the sun had bleached it like Bunny's bones. She couldn't figure the woman's age. Old enough to be her sister? Mother? Grandmother?

The mare snorted. The woman looked Clara in the eye, looked clear down into her soul. "I guess I better get you back to the house."

* * *

Clara stood in the yellowing grass of Wiley Creek. It had become her custom to watch for the painted ponies each evening, between supper and driving Pearl into town. She never witnessed their dancing and cavorting again, however.

Pearl called out from the barn, "It's getting late."

Clara turned away from the promise of ponies. She was disappointed and told Pearl so.

"They show up when they're needed," was Pearl's answer. Clara didn't know what that meant, as the ponies seemed to serve no true purpose, but asking Pearl questions was useless. Pearl was an odd one and didn't have a lot to say about anything.

Clara led Lulu, Pearl's brown filly, out of the barn, already hitched up to Pearl's smart black rig. Pearl stepped aboard. Clara took up the reins. Lulu, with a jaunty little high step, brought them into Carbondale, to Pearl's business enterprise, the Carbondale Grand Lodge and Saloon. Pearl took in desperate women and made money off of them. Clara didn't understand how Pearl could render assistance in the form of shelter, food, and wages and yet profit from their whoring. But asking questions on this matter proved useless as well.

At midnight, Clara handed over the stable duties to Dimwit Jericho Stutts, the only male in Pearl's employ. She went round to the back entrance, through the kitchen where Cookie always had a little something set aside for her, and headed into the saloon to buy herself a whiskey.

Gloria was at the piano, playing something rousing to promote drinking, gambling, and whoring. The saloon was full of cigar smoke, the smell of liquor, and men. Minnie appeared at the top of the stairs, adjusting her skirt. The wood creaked and complained as she eased her two-hundred-plus pounds down to the main room. A bold purple eye-patch covered her right eye and, as she descended, Minnie lifted the patch slightly and winked at Clara with her good right eye. "You gonna buy me a drink, Clark Smith?"

Clara saluted with her whiskey.

One of the miners playing poker leapt out his seat, shoutin' that "the fuckin' Eye-talian" across the table was a damn cheat. The piano notes spun off-kilter as Gloria ducked under her instrument. The suspected cheater pulled a gun and took a wild shot. There was a moment of thundering silence, then the crash of Minnie tumbling down the stairs, a trail of red in her wake.

All hell broke loose then, with the men fighting and blaming. Clara crawled toward Minnie while shots whizzed overhead. Then silence again as Pearl waded into the middle of the mayhem, shut down the place, and assured Sheriff Buckholzer that everything was fine, just fine, and she'd take care of everything. Sheriff Buckholzer hauled off the miners, probably to sleep it off in the jail and be released to go back to work in the morning.

Gloria returned to her piano, her fingers shaking. She closed the key cover.

"Get Lulu hitched up," Pearl told Clara. "I'm taking Minnie to the ranch."

"What the hell for? She's dead," Clara spit. Minnie's head was cradled in her lap. Minnie had a little boy somewhere back East, a fine son who lived in a cottage by the sea. That's what Minnie had claimed, anyway. Who was going to tell him his mama'd been shot over a damn card game? "You're not going to do anything about this? You know those miners won't spend one day in prison for killing her. Nobody gives a damn about a whore, ain't that right? Not even you?"

"Get the rig," was all Pearl said over her shoulder as she climbed the stairs.

Clara stomped and cussed her way back to the stables. Sure, her wages came from the whores, too. She was a damn hypocrite talking about the money they brought in and then taking it herself. But it just wasn't right how Pearl was handling Minnie's death. With a heavy heart and conflicted mind, Clara harnessed Lulu up and drove the rig around to the back door of the saloon. Cookie opened the door and Pearl hauled out a rolled-up carpet. It was surely too heavy for Pearl but there she was, hefting the bloated carpet into the back of the rig like Clara flung bales of hay over her shoulder.

Pearl stepped up next to Clara and looked clear down into her soul.

And Clara realized, like being kicked by a longhorn in the gut, that she wanted Pearl to see clear on down to Clarabelle.

They rode home in silence.

At the ranch, Pearl hefted the bundle and started walking. Clara followed across the dirt yard, past the barn and garden, past the farmyard, down through yellowing grass and wet of Wiley Creek. They walked past one, two, three cottonwoods stripped of leaves. Pearl nodded for Clara to stay put. She walked a bit further, then laid Minnie down and unrolled her carpet shroud.

Tears gathered in Clara's eyes. Minnie used to tease her, "How about a free ride, Clark?" Clara would always laugh and toss back a whiskey because neither men nor women had ever much appealed to her, and Minnie hadn't cared about that one bit.

The sound of bells came gently from the East, just a sense of jingling at first, just a suggestion, then more and louder until there was no mistaking them. Clara turned and there they were—the Painted Ponies running, jumping, dancing across the desert, through the sage and bitterbrush. They came as if bidden by Pearl. But that thinking was wrong. It wasn't Pearl that drew them.

The lead mare approached with don't-mess-with-me steps, always wary, always suspicious, always protecting.

She sniffed the fabric smudged with blood and the stained lace that lifted like worn daisy petals in the breeze. The scent of roses and carbolic acid rose up. The mare's teeth chomped. Her ears flicked. She stomped her foot and the bells jangled.

The fabric jerked.

A low nicker—a foal's call—then a hoof, golden and sharp, kicked out from under the dirty petticoat. The herd paced. There was a scrambling, then another foal-call to the lead mare, who offered up a mare-call. The fabric fell away as a plum-colored filly with a white spot around her right eye shook off fabric and lace, left boots behind, and struggled on her new thin legs. The filly staggered, tripped, kicked up her heels, twirled and rolled in the muck of the creek. The other ponies nuzzled and nosed her, committed her scent to memory. Then the lead mare guided the painted ponies back up the arroyo, never looking back at Pearl or Clara or the blood and stench of the brothels.

* * *

"Clark?" The male voice was coarse from trail dust and saloon smoke. "I'll be damned, it is you."

Clara pulled her persona tight as a corset and turned to face the old man in the livery doorway. She tried to remember how men talked to each other. The words. The tone. She had to dig deep to remember. "How the hell are ya, Franklin?"

"Good. Good."

Franklin's mule, Matilda, stood behind him staring blankly out to some unknown horizon. She did that sometimes. Clark always wondered what she was looking at but never did figure it out. Bunny had loved Matilda, and the feeling had seemed mutual. Whenever Franklin joined them on the trail—Matilda hauling the supply wagon—Bunny'd prefer to be with the mule at the end of the day than with the other horses. They'd murmur to each other in the dark and sleep side by side.

For a moment, Clara felt the presence of the little gray mare. But she was gone, she reminded herself. The thought of seeing the blank space where Bunny shoulda been kept her from looking back. It still hurt. If only she hadn't…

Franklin stroked his yellowing beard. "Heard you was goin' west to California to breed horses or some such nonsense."

"That's the plan."

"Not surprised. Sure, you always did have a way with the ponies. Looks like you didn't get far."

"Winter came on me."

Franklin nodded and spit on the ground between them. It left a nasty blotch in the dirt. "Plenty warm enough now. Me and Matilda are going to Frisco. Got a cousin lives out there. He needs strong men to work the docks. We should travel together. Where's your pony? Rabbit, was it?"

"Bunny."

"Yeah, that's right. What grown man calls his pony Bunny?" He spit again.

"She died."

"Ah, well, I'm sorry 'bout that." He removed his hat for a moment. There was a second of silence. The loss of a good trail horse, one that had served well, was always respected by the men even after they drove their horses to that death. It was strange. Franklin replaced his hat and handed over Matilda's reins. "If you're comin', be ready in the morning. Be good to have an extra set of eyes looking out for danger. But for now," Franklin made a show of winking, "a hot bath and a whore'll fix me up right before that last push to the Pacific."

"I'll think on it."

Franklin walked off to the saloon, leaving Clara with Matilda and a decision to make.

Franklin was right, traveling together would be safer. But the thought of going west…it just didn't set as well as it had under last summer's sun. As she lead Matilda to an empty stall, the old mule laid her jaw over her shoulder and blew out a breath. Bunny'd always done the same. Then Matilda stumbled, caught herself, and plodded forward, never losing that blank stare. The poor mule would never see Frisco. She deserved to die in a thick bed of hay, not on the trail where she'd end up no better than Bunny.

Clara's mind turned the thoughts over. Franklin was shrewd when it came to taking advantage of a situation.

He'd hold out until Clara offered enough to buy a sturdy trail horse to replace the old mule. Clara had a little money stashed away. Whore money. To buy the freedom of an old mule. She wondered what Minnie would think of it. And if she left in the morning with Franklin, she'd need a horse of her own. She added up the money she'd saved. It might work. Then she'd leave Matilda with Pearl. Surely she had enough room for one more. And head West to that dream she'd had since she was Clarabelle, following her daddy around the stables.

At midnight, Clara handed over the stable duties to Jericho and headed into the saloon for a word with Pearl. But when Clara got to Pearl's office on the second floor, she was face down at her desk, columns of numbers crawling like ants beneath her cheek. At first, Clara thought she was asleep. One touch to her cheek proved Clara wrong.

At the ranch, Clara hefted the rolled-up carpet that contained Pearl Wiley up onto her shoulder and walked across the dirt yard, past the barn and garden, through the new green grass and wet of Wiley Creek. She walked past one, two, three cottonwoods with hopeful budding leaves. She walked a bit further and laid Pearl down.

The sound of bells came gently from the East, just a sense of jingling at first, just a suggestion, then more and louder until there was no mistaking them. There was the unfurling of the carpet, the nickering and whinnying, the rustle of fabric. A silver filly, pale as the moon danced as lithe and strong as a prima ballerina. Then all the Painted Ponies looked clear on down into Clara's soul.

And Clara realized that they could see clear on down to Clarabelle Cariveau.

"I guess I'll be staying here."

The lead mare snorted and tossed her head, then spun and lead them all back up the arroyo, never looking back, the new silver filly glowing like moonlight.

As Clara turned to leave, a flash of white caught her attention. She leaned over the slow water of Wiley Creek. Pearl's face gazed back at her, silver hair and clear eyes and skin as white as bones bleached by the sun. Bunny laid her jaw across Clara's shoulder and blew out a breath.

"Ain't life full of surprises?" Clara asked her little gray pony. "It's kind of like raising up horses. Don't you think?"

* * *

Every now and again, the teenaged boys of Carbondale, when they got themselves all riled up and drunk, would declare that they was goin' out and gettin' themselves a Painted Pony. They'd clamber into jacked-up pickups and crank up the radio, and thunder off into the desert, nearly falling out of the truck beds. In the morning, they'd come crawling back with headaches and stories 'bout seeing the sparks of silver hooves in the dark, and swearin' they'd heard laughter and piano music echoing through the canyons. Once, Chad Bradley woke up in the middle of the football field with a hoof print on his forehead and no memories of the past three days as proof of such things.

On those mornings, Ms. Pearl Wiley would emerge from the office of her fine establishment on Main Street, on the opposite end of town from the First Church of Christ Our Savior and grab a latte at the Starbucks on the corner. She'd shake her head, then shake the hand of her financial advisor, review the income and expenses, and hire more staff at a livable wage. She'd fire up her candy apple red 1969 Corvette and drive on out to her place—a five hundred acre spread that many a man had offered to buy for oil drilling or data storage. Pearl Wiley had no use for the money they threw at her, discovering long ago that women would always come to the Carbondale Lodge & Spa looking for a new life. She, being the sole proprietor, kept her properties intact and, when the time was right, she watched for the Painted Ponies of Wiley Creek.

About the Authors

Maren Bradley Anderson is a writer, teacher, and alpaca rancher in Oregon. She teaches English at Western Oregon University. She fills her days caring for alpacas, playing with her kids, and reading books that make her laugh. She has written two plays for the Apple Box Children's Theater, and her writing has appeared in *The Timberline Review*, *Alpacas Magazine*, and *The Christian Science Monitor*. Her novels *Fuzzy Logic* and *Closing the Store* are available online and through your local bookstore—just ask them to order them for you.

Elizabeth Beechwood is your typical Subaru-driving, scarf-knitting, bird-feeding tree hugger who lives on the fringes of Portland, Oregon. When she writes, she begins by focusing on regular people with regular lives...but then something strange happens. She earned an MFA in Popular Fiction at the University of Southern Maine's Stonecoast program and her fiction has been featured in Crossed Genres and Every Day Fiction.
You can visit her at www.elizabethbeechwood.com.

Taylor Buccello is a senior at Central High School. She lives in Monmouth, Oregon, with her parents, two bulldogs, coatimundi, lemur, and two tortoises. She mostly writes action, fantasy, and horror YA stories. She is currently writing an assassin novel she hopes to have finished before attending university in the fall of 2019. She aspires to be a published author and forensic pathologist.

Rosie Bueford is a wife, a mother, a social worker in the making. She currently attends Portland State University studying in the Social Work program. She serves her community with her career at DHS. Rosie loves to travel and study other cultures. She is passionate about connecting to the lives and stories of diverse, unique, beautiful people. She loves to express her own life experiences through her music, writing and art.

Lizzy Carney is a member of Society of Children's Book Writers and Illustrators and The Willamette Writers. She belongs to two critique groups and attends regional writer conferences. She enjoys writing in a variety of genres. Her essay "Death Stalks My Mother" was published as part of the anthology *Upon Arrival of Illness: Coming to Terms with the Dark Companion* (Savage Press 2012). Presently, she is working on picture book manuscripts and a book for Alzheimer's caregivers. The working title is: *Beyond Pee, Poop and Pills. The Life of an Alzheimer's Caregiver*.

Sydney Culpepper self-published her first novel, *Pagetown,* as part of her high school senior project. She graduated from Western Oregon University with a degree in linguistics and an honors thesis titled *Young People Are Always On Their Phones: A Sociolinguistic Analysis of Text Messaging*. She spends her days trying to balance her many passions and hobbies, including working on her next book. Sydney has also worked as an editor for Not a Pipe Publishing since 2017.

Debby Dodds is the author of the novel *Amish Guys Don't Call* (Blue Moon, June 2017) which was awarded "One of the Best YA of 2017" by Powell's Books. She has stories in ten anthologies, including the NY Times best-selling *My Little Red Book* (Hachette) and *The Things That You Would Have Said* (Penguin) as well as: *The Sun, Salon.com, xoJane, The Living Dead Magazine,* and *Hip Mama,* and she won Portland's Wizard World 2017 Fiction Contest. She used to be known for her screams in horror movies and her "melting routine" onstage at Disney World.

Karen Eisenbrey lives in Seattle, WA, where she leads a quiet, orderly life and invents stories to make up for it. Karen writes fantasy and science fiction novels, as well as short fiction in a variety of genres and the occasional poem if it insists. She also sings in a church choir, plays drums and sings backup in a garage band, and was surprised to find herself writing songs for her debut YA novel *The Gospel According to St. Rage* (Pankhearst, 2016). She shares her life with her husband, two young adult sons, and two mature adult cats.

Julia Figliotti is a published writer with a wide range of publications. She has authored several books and articles on creativity, as well as fictional short stories and poetry. Julia has a Bachelor's degree in Writing from SUNY Buffalo State and a Master's degree in Creativity from the International Center for Studies in Creativity. She spent several years working with facilitators of scientific workshops. Now a full-time writer, Julia works to bring visions to life on paper. She is currently working on publishing her first children's story (which is absolutely nothing like "Skin-Deep").

Claudine Griggs is the Writing Center Director at Rhode Island College, and her publications include three nonfiction books about transsexuals along with a couple dozen articles on writing, teaching, and other topics. She also writes fiction and science fiction, her first-love genre as a teenager. Griggs earned her BA and MA in English at California State Polytechnic University, Pomona.

Chloe Hagerman was born in Portland in 1989, and although she attended Knox College in Illinois and has lived and traveled around the world, she still calls Portland her home. She has been writing since she was 11, and has always striven to better her works with the help and support of friends and family. She prefers writing fiction, from short stories to plays to full-length novels. Her story "Warriors of Sukra" is available on Amazon.

Jean Harkin, of Washington County, Oregon, is the author of "Night in Alcatraz: And Other Uncanny Tales," an anthology of short stories honed by magic realism and humor, published in 2016. She belongs to two writers' groups: Writers' Mill in Portland and Northwest Independent Writers Association. She is revising her novel, "Promise Full of Thorns" that was selected as a finalist in Maple Lane Books publishing contest, 2016.

Laura Hazan is a librarian with the Enoch Pratt Free Library where she runs the bimonthly Light Street Writers Exchange. She completed her first novel, *Little Boxes*, and is still seeking representation for publication. She has a B.A. in communications from American University, a M.L.S. in Library Science from the University of Maryland, and attended the "Your Novel Year" program at Arizona State University's Piper Writing Center. She is a resident of Baltimore and lives with her son, her husband, and their one-eyed dog named, what else, Boh.

Tonya Lippert is the co-author of *TRANSFORMING ADHD* (New Harbinger Publications), a non-fiction book for adults, and the author of the picture book *Goodbye, School* (Magination Press), which is scheduled to be out early 2019. She has a Ph.D. and M.S. which focus her attention on mental health and child abuse. When she first moved to Portland, she taught at Reed College as a visiting professor and worked at the Oregon Social Learning Center. A mother of two, she loves traveling the world with her children.

M.K. Martin is the author of the science fiction action novel *The Survivor's Club,* which was released by Not a Pipe Publishing in the spring of 2018. Martin has published a couple of short stories as part of the Veterans' Writing Project and a personal essay in the anthology *So Glad They Told Me*. In 2015, she received Honorable Mention from The Writers of the Future Q4 contest for her short story "Awakenings." She currently resides in the Pacific Northwest with her soulmate, their future astronaut daughter, and obligatory evil cat. When not writing, she enjoys tea, video games, and reading (of course!).

Growing up in Fort Worth, Texas, **LeeAnn Elwood McLennan** was always looking for any opportunity to read—under the covers in bed, in the car, and even in class. Stories permeate her life from her multiple Alice in Wonderland tattoos to the names of her cats (Atticus, Boo Radley, and Finch). Though she graduated from Clemson University with a degree in English, LeeAnn has spent her career working in computer engineering related fields. LeeAnn lives in Portland, Oregon with her husband, Andy, and three cats (number of cats subject to change).

Life as a middle school science teacher for twenty-four years has allowed **Heather S. Ransom** an intimate look into the minds of thousands of young adults, most of whom are desperate to find their place in society. Many have found escape, ideas for facing challenges, or simply hope for a future where they can make a difference, through reading. So every year, even though she's teaching science, Heather has her classes read. When not teaching or writing, Heather enjoys spending time with the man of her dreams, Marv, and their two absolutely amazing adult kids, Danielle and Marvin.

An out lesbian since adolescence, **Lori Ubell**'s own experiences inform this story. She studied writing with James Frey (*How to Write a Damn Good Novel*), Dorothy Allison and Emily Whitman. She belongs to a critique group which meets twice a month and has been on-going for about two years. She's am an active member of SCBWI, Willamette Writers, and the Historical Novel Society. She's published poetry, short stories and non-fiction in both regional and national publications, including *Parade*, *Hadassah*, *Lilith*, and *The Oregonian.*

Also Available from Not a Pipe Publishing

Shadow Girl

by

Kate Ristau

Áine lives in the light, but she is haunted by darkness, and when her fey powers blaze out of control, she escapes into the Shadowlands. But she cannot outrun her past. Fire fey and a rising darkness threaten the light, burning a path across the veil. Her fiery dreams come to life, and with the help of Hennessy, an uninhibited Irish girl, Áine dives into the flames to discover who she truly is. Her mother burned to keep her secret safe, and now Áine wields the deadly Eta. She must learn to fight in the shadows – or die in the flames.

This is not a fairy tale.

"A fun, engaging, and unique magical adventure."
-Jen Violi
author of *Putting Makeup on Dead People*

Wherever Fine Books Are Sold

CPSIA information can be obtained
at www.ICGtesting.com
Printed in the USA
FFHW020257221118
49538178-53914FF

9 781948 120241